SHABBAT SABOTAGE

EMMA CARLSON BERNE

YELLOW
JACKET

 **YELLOW JACKET**
an imprint of Little Bee Books

New York, NY
Text Copyright © 2022 by Emma Carlson Berne
Illustrations by Kayla Stark
All rights reserved, including the right of
reproduction in whole or in part in any form.
Yellow Jacket and associated colophon are
trademarks of Little Bee Books.
Interior designed by Natalie Padberg Bartoo
Manufactured in the United States of America VEP 1221
First Edition
10 9 8 7 6 5 4 3 2 1
Library of Congress Cataloging-in-Publication
Data is available upon request.
ISBN 978-1-4998-1307-4 (hc)
ISBN 978-1-4998-1308-1 (ebook)
littlebeebooks.com
For information about special discounts on bulk purchases,
please contact Little Bee Books at sales@littlebeebooks.com.

For the campers and staff
of Camp Livingston.—E.C.B.

PROLOGUE

"You're all set!" Mom barged into Maya's room, holding a folded sheet of paper. Maya looked up from *Lord of the Flies*. They were just about to sacrifice Piggy. Through her window, Maya could see snow falling thickly, illuminated by the Millers' garage light. Maybe they'd cancel school tomorrow.

"Set with what?" Maya marked her place in the book with her finger and sat up. She tried to look patient.

"Camp!" Mom read from the paper. "We are so pleased to welcome you to your first summer at Camp Shalom. This all-girls sleepaway camp offers campers a summer packed with unique camp activities and a solid grounding in Jewish culture."

"I already have a solid grounding in Jewish culture." Maya took the paper Mom offered. "I'm super grounded."

The paper read:

WELCOME TO YOUR CAMP SHALOM SUMMER!

Get ready for friendship and fun!

Kayaking

Daily swimming

Campcraft

Giant water slide

Animal care and nature study

Kosher meals

All-camp bonfires

Sports and games in the meadow

Shabbat by the lake

. . . and that's just the beginning!

Maya tried to hand the paper back, but Mom wouldn't take it. They were really going to make her go. "Mom, please, I really don't think Camp Shalom is for me." She'd only said it like five hundred times.

Mom got that look on her face, and Maya knew it was hopeless. Here came a pep talk. "Honey, you need to try. You need to push yourself. Otherwise, you'll just stay in your room the whole summer. You need to engage with the outside world. Taking on your fears is important, and I know you can do it!"

"Mom, you know I hate pep talks. Please don't." Maya thrust the paper at her mother and curled up like a pill bug. She pulled her pillow over her head.

Her mother's voice was resolute. "We didn't send

you last year, but this was our agreement. This year is the year." She dropped the paper on top of the pillow and went out, closing the door behind her.

Maya pulled up her sweatshirt hood and lay back on the bed, ignoring the crinkle of the paper underneath her. She crossed her hands on her stomach and stared at the ceiling. In five months, she was going to summer camp. She didn't want to sleep in bunk beds with strangers snoring or eat smelly cafeteria food. She wanted to stay home, in her room, where everything was perfect. Maya closed her eyes. She didn't have to look to see her books all arranged by author on the shelves, or her lap desk for drawing and her glass animals and her white dresser with the fancy mirror Mom found at a garage sale. Everything hers, everything safe.

Daily swimming.

She tried to shove the words out of her mind. At least she had the rest of the winter and spring. Cabins and cold showers and kayaks seemed so far away from reality right now. Maybe Mom and Dad would forget. Maybe there would be an earthquake and Camp Shalom would fall into a sinkhole. Maya rolled over on her stomach and opened *Lord of the Flies* again. Outside, the snow kept falling.

CHAPTER 1

The camp bus swung around another curve, and Maya's stomach rose. She closed her eyes. She really didn't want to lose her lunch in front of all these kids before camp had even started. The bus was hot and smelled like diesel fuel and plastic and bananas. Maya wiggled in the cracked vinyl seat. She was so sweaty, even her underwear felt damp.

Camp Shalom had not sunk into a sinkhole or imploded or been dismantled plank-by-plank by a disgruntled former camper. She had not gotten her wish, and the plans for camp had gone forward like some kind of machine set in motion, the kind with lots of pulleys and gears. Cabin lists came in the mail, along with piles of forms and a camper handbook the size of a brick. Two giant black duffel bags had appeared on her bedroom floor, and Mom had filled them with pillows, special extra-long sheets, two new bathing suits, a shower caddy, shower shoes, and free stationery from the public library for writing home. Piles of T-shirts. Piles of shorts. A pack of new socks. A little framed picture of her, Mom, and Dad all sitting in one big chair. Would that even be enough for seven weeks away?

Maya's throat swelled a little, thinking of the picture, stuffed somewhere in one of her giant duffels, which was in turn stuffed somewhere under the bus, along with everyone else's giant duffels. And then, after a lazy curve in the road . . . there was the lake. The lake! The lake! She'd seen it when she she'd driven up with Mom and Dad to visit. They'd wanted to show her Camp Shalom itself, hoping it would change her attitude. It didn't. The lake was so . . . big. And dark. She imagined gnarly fish lurking under its murky surface. And did eels live in lakes? She couldn't remember. Either way, it looked perfect for drowning. Perfect for her own drowning.

Maya didn't know anyone at camp, so no one knew her secret. No one knew what had happened to her the previous summer at the pool.

She'd been at the big, noisy rec center day camp. It wasn't fun. The kids were too wild, and no one listened to the counselors. There were sports, so it was like gym class but all summer. Torture, in other words. She mostly tried to hang around with her friend Becky, who was good at swimming and kickball. Becky was kind of her protector. But at swimming one day, when Becky wasn't there, she sat on the edge of the pool, by the deep end, cooling her feet in the water. A boy named Miles, who had blond hair and was obsessed with soccer, walked by, and she'd felt his hand thump her back. For one instant, she thought he was giving her some kind of playful punch, and since she'd always had a tiny crush on him, that was great. But then, in the next instant, she realized he was pushing her into the pool.

The water gave her a cold shock all over her body, forcing the air out of her lungs. It closed in around her head. Her feet couldn't find the bottom. She tried to gasp for air, but the water was like a trap around her. She gulped, swallowing mouthfuls of chlorinated water.

She tried to break to the surface and caught a sliver of air. She could see kids running on the edge of the pool in the sun, and others standing and talking. No one noticed her. She tried to yell, but only a cough of water came out. *I'm drowning*, she thought. *I'm really drowning. This is how it feels to drown. All the drowned people, this is how they felt, only they never got to come back to tell us how it feels. It's really happening.*

But then she felt someone's arm wrap around her ribs. The arm practically jerked her out of the water, and then a rubbery thing was thrust into her arms. "It's okay, I've got you," a girl's voice said. It was the lifeguard. Maya had clung to the float, gasping and squeezing it while the lifeguard towed her to the side of the pool. She could hardly believe she wasn't dead. Instead, she was sitting on a pool chair, wrapped in a yellow towel, shivering and crying, while a silent crowd of kids stood around and stared. Miles stood at the back, staring too. Maya didn't look at his face. She didn't want to see if he was sorry or not. It was better not to know.

That was it for swimming. She never got back into the pool, and her mom wrote a note excusing her. "But this is your chance to really start facing your fear!" Mom said when they came for visiting day and saw the lake. "You have to push yourself!"

She kind of hated pushing herself. No, she *really* hated pushing herself. But Mom and Dad were very into facing their fears. It was a thing with them. They themselves weren't afraid of anything, and there was no reason Maya should be either. That's what they said, at least.

Except she was. Terribly afraid. And now she was here. There weren't any excuse notes, and the lake wasn't going anywhere.

A clatter across the aisle jerked Maya out of her thoughts. A girl in a drapey gray T-shirt and leggings had dropped a little case of bobby pins. Maya had already noticed her. She'd gotten on the bus at a stop about an hour earlier, and immediately Maya regretted wearing her Glendale Fun Run T-shirt with the orange juice stain. The girl had that kind of thick black hair that hung like a curtain. It draped halfway down her back, with waves and ripples. Maya had always wanted that kind of hair. Her own thinnish, wavyish light-brownish hair was so . . . *wavery*. It never did what she wanted. In class, she'd watch the girls with hair like this girl. They take all their hair, just so casually, swirl it up on top of their heads, stick a pencil in it or wrap a hairband around it, and there it would be, just this perfect messy bun, smack on top of their heads, with little pieces hanging down. And she'd try the same thing at home, and her hair just wouldn't do it. Weird bumps would stick out, and she'd get so mad that she wanted to smash the mirror and shave her head.

The girl with the amazing hair muttered something and leaned over to pick up her mess. But at the same time, Maya swooped down to help her. Their heads collided with a sharp crack.

"*Ow!*" The girl straightened up, rubbing her forehead. "Watch it!" Her voice was loud enough that several other kids looked up.

"Sorry!" Maya said, grabbing her own head. "I was, *um*, just trying to get your pins."

"Well, you smacked my head instead," the girl snapped. "I can get them fine by myself." She eyed Maya for a long moment. Maya crossed her arms over the juice stain. She really should have changed after this morning's spill.

Maya nodded and shrank back into the corner of her seat. She watched the girl gather up her hair into a big, swirly twist, then poke the long bobby pins in one by one. She made it look so easy.

A girl sitting behind Maya reached over the seat and tapped her on the shoulder. "Do you want some gum?" she asked. "Pass it on." She had a round, cheerful face, and eyebrows so thick they looked like caterpillars. Beside her sat a girl with bouncy dark curls and glasses who was pawing through her backpack, looking worried.

"Thanks." Maya took the plastic canister of gum. It was cinnamon Ice Cubes. "This is my favorite kind," she told the eyebrow girl.

"Me too! Did you ever get all the flavors at once? My big sister gave me that for my last birthday." She grinned at Maya, and Maya smiled back. She seemed nice. Maybe they'd be in the same cabin.

"I'm Annie, by the way," eyebrow girl said. "Rachel and I are from Louisville." She indicated the girl next to her.

"I think I left my allergy spray at home." Rachel looked up from her backpack. "I really need it." Her forehead was all crinkled with worry.

"Let's just ask the counselor what to do when we get off the bus," Annie said, and gave a Maya a little eye-roll look.

Maya smiled back and faced forward. Maybe, if she and Annie were in the same cabin, they could share a bunk.

The bus caravan turned onto a smaller, dirt road. Mechanical gates rolled back, and the bus rumbled through. Maya could see a big lawn spreading out ahead, filled with maybe fifty people. They all looked like counselors or staff. That made sense because all the campers were on the bus. Their bright T-shirts were a rainbow of color against the green grass. Behind them, Maya noticed a low wooden building that must be the office, and then the gravel paths branching off that led to the rest of the camp concealed behind the trees.

The bus ground to a halt, and the driver turned off the engine and opened the doors. A tanned guy with dark hair and a clipboard bounded onto the bus. "Welcome to Camp Shalom!" he shouted. The bus erupted in cheers and clapping. Maya clapped, too, but she wasn't sure she meant it. "I'm Max, the camp director! Get ready for your official camp entrance!"

Outside the bus windows, Maya could see the mass of rainbow-clad people surging toward the bus. They were lining up on either side of the bus doors and putting their arms up and together, making an arm-tunnel. Everyone on the bus stood up and started talking and gathering their things.

Maya slid as far down in her seat as she could. Maybe if she stayed very still, the counselor would think she was dead and leave her there. That might actually be preferable to getting off the bus and having all those people looking at her and shouting. Having to meet all of them, all those new people at once . . . sticking a hot pin through her own eye would be preferable, now that she thought about it.

"*Um*, what are you doing?" the bobby-pin girl asked, standing up gracefully and slinging a backpack over her shoulder. Her voice held that unmistakable popular-girl trill. It was like a thing with them, Maya had figured out. They talked that way so they could recognize each other in the wild. Kind of like whales singing.

Maya sat up straight and grabbed her own backpack. "I just . . . dropped my headphones," she said, making up an excuse for not getting up with everyone else. She edged out of the seat and shuffled down the aisle, smooshing against the other campers. She resisted the urge to unstick her sweaty underwear from her rear end.

A cheer rose from the counselors as the first campers bounded down the bus steps. Everyone was singing. "*Welcome, welcome, we're glad you're here! Welcome, welcome to you! A big Camp Shaaaalommm welcome—to you!*" Maya tried to smile like everyone else. Annie and Rachel had disappeared into the crowd. She could see the swirly haired girl up in front of her. She crouched down as she ran through the arm tunnel, all the faces leaning down to peer at her. It was really corny, but honestly, a little fun too. Then she was through. This was it. She'd officially arrived at her brand-new sleepaway camp—Camp Shalom.

The counselors were mostly tanned and looked like college students. Some older people, Maya guessed, ran the camp. They were all wearing rainbow tie-dyed Camp Shalom T-shirts. A lot of them had on sandals on their feet and bandannas around their heads and many wore braids.

"Welcome, campers!" a voice echoed out from above. Max was standing on a big rock, holding a megaphone. "Time for cabin-sorting! Remember that at Shalom, all the cabins are named for places in Israel, so listen up!"

Maya shuffled aside, clutching her backpack. She felt like a sheep. A scared sheep. She tried to look for Annie and her big eyebrows, but she couldn't see her in the crush.

The counselors all lined up in front, with papers in their hands. Fast, Maya tried to decide who looked the nicest. The one with the long brown hair, she decided, and the big smile. She crossed her fingers she'd get that cabin.

A short, stocky girl with a hard face stepped forward. "Eilat! Eilat campers are . . ." She started reading from a list. Older girls crowded forward, and Maya started focusing on the next group. The campers pressed all around her smelled like sunscreen and sweat and powdery deodorant. She craned her head. The nice-looking counselor was calling out names now. "Haifa! The Haifas are . . ." She read from her list, and Annie ran over to her, then Rachel.

Please, please, Maya thought, crossing her fingers so tightly, she ground the bones together.

Then the Haifa counselor folded her paper. That was it. Somehow, Maya felt even more alone than before, as if Annie had abandoned some unspoken contract they had.

"Akko! Listen for your name, Akkos!" a blonde counselor at the front was calling. She had short hair, shaved on the sides and the back, and she was tanned, with strong-looking arms. "Maya Peck! Dani Bogale! Gracie Klein!"

The rest of the names were lost in the noise as Maya trundled over to the blonde counselor. The camper standing next to her was trying to keep hold of her giant purple sleeping bag, which was slipping out of its covering.

"Oh, here," Maya said. She tried to help gather up the slippery nylon folds.

"Thanks," the girl said, sounding a little out of breath. "It started slipping when I was getting off the bus. I'm Dani, by the way." Dani's hair was swept back in a high ponytail. She had a wide, open smile.

"Are you from Detroit too?" Maya asked.

Dani shook her head. "I'm from Cincinnati. My mom used to go here, so of course, she wanted me to go too, at, like, the first possible minute. It's my first summer."

"Me too. I've just been to day camp before at the J." Maya noticed a paperback of Sherlock Holmes stories sticking out of her sweatshirt pocket. "Hey, I know that guy!" she said. "We read *The Hound of the Baskervilles* in school."

Dani pulled the paperback out. "Holmes is my absolute favorite," she said. "He's a crazy genius. He uses the tiniest clues to figure out a mystery."

"All right, everyone, listen up!" the counselor said. "I'm Tamar. I'm the Akko counselor. We'll do more intros later. Let's see who's here."

Maya could tell Tamar was going to be one of those tough camp counselors. She'd had them at day camp. They knew how to build different kinds of fires and gave you the side-eye if you scraped yourself and cried a little.

Tamar looked at her clipboard. "Maya?"

"Here!" Maya said.

"Dani?"

"Here!"

The other two girls were Gracie and Marisa. They were both from Indianapolis, and they'd both been to camp before.

"We're just missing one person," Tamar said, "Yael Rosen. Anyone seen her?"

"Here! Wait, I'm here!" someone said. Maya turned around. The bobby-pin girl was struggling up beside them, dragging a huge duffel. *Great.* Maya edged behind Dani, hoping Yael wouldn't see her, even though Dani was built like a pencil.

"Sorry!" Yael declared. "They couldn't find my bag! Then they found it, but it had come unzipped, so the driver helped me put everything back in. Anyway, do you have any ibuprofen? I think I'm getting a migraine. I get them, you know, and—"

Tamar blinked. "We're not allowed to give out medication," she said. "You'll have to go to the nurse's hut for that."

"Oh, okay!" Yael said. "It's just that some clumsy girl headbutted me on the bus, and it really hurt—oh, hello!" She spotted Maya. "That's the girl," she said to the group, all of whom were watching.

Maya nodded like an idiot and wondered if her playing-dead bus plan would still work. She could just have a small heart attack. It would be painless.

"Too bad you didn't hit her harder. Then maybe she'd be quiet," Dani murmured beside her.

Maya glanced over, and Dani gave her a little sideways grin. One of her incisors was chipped at an angle. Dani glared at Yael, then rolled her eyes deliberately.

"Are you sharing a bunk yet with anyone?" Dani asked. "Want to share?"

"Yeah!" Maya let herself smile. It felt good. She may have messed up with Yael—but at least she already had a new friend.

CHAPTER 2

"Let's go find our cabin!" Tamar called. "We'll do a camp tour on the way. You can leave your duffels and sleeping bags here. The gator will bring them around later." She marched ahead as everyone grabbed their duffels and sleeping bags and staggered after her. *What's a gator?* Maya wondered. They were walking away from the office on the gravel path, which wove through a grove of oak and pine trees. The air felt different from at home, even though she was only a few hours away. Maybe forest air always felt like this? It was cooler and crisp.

"This is the *chadar ochel*," Tamar said as they approached a big wooden building with screens halfway up the walls.

"What's that?" Marisa asked. "What's a chadar?" She pronounced it "chaddar," sort of like the cheese.

"The dining hall," Tamar said. They crowded the door, peeking in. Maya saw a vast, vaulted space with long tables and benches stretching from end to end. A kitchen pass-through was at one end, like at school, and at the front, a mic and a music stand were set on a small platform. "We usually have songs during meals," Tamar explained.

Another group crowded behind them, trying to look, and Tamar led them around the building to an entrance on the other side. A tree stood beside this door—or at least, it looked like a tree. It was covered with little colored bumps all over the trunk and branches. Everyone peered at it. Upon closer inspection, Maya could see that the bumps were gum—every kind and shade of gum that ever existed, gnarled into a million chewed shapes.

"And this is the gum tree," Tamar said proudly. "Camp Shalom tradition. People stick their gum on it before they go into the chadar ochel."

"Gross!" Yael said.

Secretly, Maya felt sorry for the tree, standing there pathetically with the gum stuck all over it. She gave the trunk a secret little pat as Tamar led them farther down the path. The counselor turned off onto a smaller one, carpeted in pine needles. The trees were thicker here, and the pine needles muffled their footsteps. Maya could see another group farther up and one behind them.

They passed several log cabin and screen-type

buildings, a gaga pit, tennis courts, and a big open space with logs arranged like seats. There was an open-air shack with paintbrushes in rows of jars and lanyard string hanging from hooks like fringe. Then Maya saw a group of tiny buildings standing among a grove of big pine trees.

Tamar stopped in front of a bigger building. "Shower house and bathroom." She stood aside and let the girls file in and peek.

The floor was concrete, and the walls were wood. It smelled damp and humid. A couple of older girls were standing in front of the sinks, talking while they washed their hands. There was a row of toilet stalls and a row of shower stalls. Maya breathed a little sigh of relief when she saw the showers had curtains. She wouldn't have to shower in front of everyone, thank goodness. The trash cans were big metal barrels, and the floor had a drain in the middle.

Yael stood looking at the shower stalls sadly. "At least I remembered shower shoes," she said, even though no one had asked.

Gracie didn't even bother to look in. She seemed like the super-low maintenance type. Marisa rushed into one of the stalls and banged the door. She must have *really* had to go.

"It's pretty basic," Tamar said. "Showers are every night before bed. You can go to the bathroom whenever you want, but just let me know, so I don't lose track of you, okay?"

The cabins were arranged in a horseshoe shape around a little central grassy spot, with the woods pressing in from all sides. Overhead, the oak trees rustled their thick leaves, and Maya was suddenly reminded that when she was little, she always thought the sound was rain.

A kind of souped-up green golf cart was parked in the middle of the horseshoe, piled high with duffels and sleeping bags. *That must be the gator*, Maya thought. Every cabin had screen windows and a porch that stretched across the whole front. The place was buzzing with counselors calling out and girls heaving their bags through doors. One girl crouched on the path, picking up bottles and jars that had clearly spilled from her bag. Maya picked up a soap container and handed it to her before hurrying over to the gator and thumping her own two black duffels onto the ground.

She crowded onto the porch with everyone else, and Tamar pushed open the door. "Home sweet home!" she declared. "Welcome, Akkos!"

The girls erupted in screams as everyone registered the presence of a giant black snake lying across one of the bunk beds. It had to be as long as Maya and as thick as her arm.

"Shoot! Hang on, everyone!" Tamar darted forward. "It's just a ratsnake! Harmless!" She seized a broom from behind the door and gently poked the snake.

Everyone screamed again as the snake poured itself onto the floor and slithered into a corner, as if it were trying to hide itself. Gracie shrieked. Dani looked like she was either going to cry or throw up. The snake slithered toward Yael, who avoided it with a nimble hop, and then it moved gracefully across the doorsill, nearly slithering over Maya's sneakers. She stood rooted and only dimly registered the faint diamond pattern on its smoothly muscled, scaly skin before it was over the edge of the porch, then gone.

Maya let out a breath she didn't realize she'd been holding, and everyone burst into chatter. Marisa was actually clinging to Gracie, as if to support her own legs.

"I thought it was a stick!" Yael declared. "Like a giant stick!"

"I didn't know what it was," Gracie said. She detached Marisa's hands from her arm and started dragging her duffel across the floor.

"I knew. We have them at home. They love the woodpile." Dani seized her bags.

"Nothing to worry about!" Tamar surveyed them with her hands on her hips. "Let's get unpacked, and then we'll decorate our bunks while we do introductions."

Maya had a feeling that "nothing to worry about" might be a familiar mantra with Tamar. Something about the hands-on-the-hips, direct-gaze combo tipped her off.

Their cabin was little and airy and smelled like pine trees. The walls went about halfway up and then screens took over. The floor was made of wooden planks—everything was planks, actually. Two sets of bunkbeds lined each wall, with one single bed in the corner. The mattresses were stripped bare. They smelled a little like a basement. Right near the door, Tamar had a single bed and a little desk next to it. Her bed was all made up with a green unzipped sleeping bag and navy pillows. A black-and-gold footlocker was pushed up against the end of the bed.

"All right, everyone, choose a bed and get unpacked," Tamar said. "Cubbies by each bunk are for your personal belongings. Clothes stay in your duffels, which you should shove under your bunk."

"How about this one?" Dani dumped her things on the set of bunks near the door, opposite Tamar's. "*Um*, do you mind if I take the top?"

"No, that's fine!" Actually Maya was hoping for the top, but she didn't want to say anything to upset her new, and possibly only, friend. Dani looked relieved though, so she didn't mind.

"Oh! Oh! Tamar!" Yael sang out at the top of her lungs.

"Would you mind if I had the single bed? I just have so many allergies, and I don't know if anyone here wears perfume, or like, really scented shampoo, but I might get a flare-up if I have to share, so I'll take this one, okay?" She'd hoisted her duffel onto the bed as she talked.

"If it makes you more comfortable, go ahead," Tamar said. "As long as no one else minds."

"Looks like she already took it," Dani muttered to Maya.

Maya rolled her eyes. "I think maybe she's a little high-maintenance."

Dani hoisted her sleeping bag up to the top, and Maya helped her drag up her duffel. Then Maya spent a long time carefully arranging her bed. First, she put on her favorite striped sheets from home, then she unzipped and laid out her purple sleeping bag on top. Her pillow was heart-shaped and pink. Mom had made it for her in first grade. Sitting on her new bed, she could see the lake clearly. It spread out blue and flat like a baking tray beyond the trees. It was really beautiful out here—even with the lake. Turning back to her duffel, Maya dug out her stack of books—*Animal Farm; Wonder; The Lion, the Witch and the Wardrobe; The Outsiders*—and carefully lined them up in the cubby nearest her head, like friends. Just seeing them there made her feel better. She ran her hand over the spines.

All around her, everyone was setting up their beds.

Gracie had taped a picture on her bedpost of herself and two curly haired boys standing on top of a mountain. She had a puffy black pillow on her bed and a pair of shower slides right beneath. She'd brought a battery-powered fan, too, which she'd expertly clipped to the end of her bed, so it faced her pillow. That seemed like a pro move. Maya wished she'd brought a fan.

Marisa, on the other hand, had just shoved her duffel bag under the bed before climbing up to her top bunk. The bag was still sticking out partway. Now, she was lying upside down off the bed's edge, winding up a yo-yo. Her sleeping bag was still zipped, too, and falling off the bunk. Yael had set up a little mirror on the window ledge by her single bed, and beside it she arranged a little tub of lip balm, a comb, and some packets of hair bands and pins. Everything very neat, all in a row.

Maya stood on the edge of her bed and craned up to see Dani. "Hey, can I come see your bed?"

Dani quickly put down something she was holding. "Sure."

Maya climbed up and arranged herself cross-legged on Dani's purple sleeping bag. It was warm from the sun pouring in the window. A small framed picture was lying on the bed. That was what Dani was holding. Maya picked it up. "Is that your mom?" A woman with dark, fluffy hair was giving a grinning Dani a big cheek kiss and a bear hug.

Dani cleared her throat. "Yeah. She gave me this to take in case I was . . ." Dani's voice trailed off.

Maya finished for her. "Homesick?"

Dani nodded and looked out the window. She looked like she might cry.

"Isn't it the worst feeling?" Maya said. "I used to get *sooo* homesick at my friend Ihno's house. It was weird because I was only sleeping over, but basically I just could not wait to leave. Like the minute I woke up in the morning, I would sneak downstairs really early and call my mom to come get me. Then I'd wait outside for her before Ihno even woke up!"

Dani looked over at Maya. The edge-of-tears look was gone. She laughed. "That's so funny. I get it, though."

"Okay!" Tamar called. "Come and sit in a circle." She had a bunch of craft stuff spread out on the floor—a pile of pennant banners, marker, glue, glitter jars, scissors.

The Akkos arranged themselves on the cabin floor. Maya made sure she was sitting next to Dani and not next to Yael. The floor was hard, and she squirmed a little.

"We're going to make pennant banners for our bunks." Tamar held one up. "Decorate each triangle so it represents something about you. Then we'll share them and use them to do our introductions, okay? For instance, here's mine." She held it up. "I've got a compass, because I like wilderness navigation, the Israeli flag, since that's where I'm from. I grew up Tel Aviv, and I was stationed in the Golan during my army service. This triangle has a tomato and a cucumber, since Israeli salad is my favorite food."

"What's Israeli salad?" Marisa asked. "A salad made of Israelis?"

Maya stifled a giggle. Marisa grinned at her.

"Tomato and cucumber chopped up together with oil and vinegar. It's pretty much the national dish of Israel." Tamar put down her banner. "Okay, take a few minutes."

The cabin fell quiet, except for the rustling of paper and the sound of cutting. It was the kind of silence that doesn't happen once everyone really knows each other. Maya tried not to look at other people's banners as she thought of what to draw. Finally, she sketched a book in one triangle, a cake in another, and a horse in a third, though the horse looked more like a dinosaur with a mane.

"Okay, everyone done?" Tamar asked after a few minutes. Maya sat back and put her marker down.

Gracie went first. She and Marisa were best friends from home, and they were both eleven, she told the group. She'd been coming to Shalom since she was eight. "I've got a pair of hiking boots on mine, because that's my favorite activity, and a tent, since I like camping, and a four, because that's how many years I've been at Shalom."

Of course, she knew to bring a fan. Maya wondered if she could maybe rope herself to Gracie if there were, like, a nuclear disaster and all civilization were destroyed and they all had to gather seeds and eat small animals raw.

"Okay, I'll go next!" Marisa tried to pick up her banner, but it ripped. "Shoot! I was sitting on it. It's okay! I'll tape it!" She held up the two pieces. "I'm Marisa, I'm from Chicago. I guess Gracie already told you that. I drew a gerbil, because I'm obsessed with them. I have two at home and one is a honey—that's the real name, and one is an agouti—she's brown, but really, really cute. And, like, I talk to them, and they listen to me, and they squeak back at me. And I drew some Hebrew letters because I'm learning to read Hebrew, but I'm not very good, and also a roller coaster because I'm on a mission to ride the biggest roller coaster I can and beat my record, which right now is the Vortex, one hundred and forty-eight feet high!"

"Okay!" Tamar said when Marisa finally sat back and took a breath. "Dani, how about you?"

"I'm from Cincinnati," Dani said when it was her turn. "I drew a book with a question mark on it because I like reading mysteries, and also a plate of Cincinnati chili. That's spaghetti with chili on top and cheese on top of that. And also a ball of yarn because I like finger knitting, and I brought some yarn if anyone wants to learn. It's really easy. And I've never been to camp before, but my mom went here. At home, I go to a Jewish day school. It's called Rockwern."

"*Um*, I'm from Detroit," Maya said when it was her turn. She held up her banner and wished she could hide behind it. "This is my first time at camp too. I like horseback riding and reading and baking—I watch this baking show with my mom every week, and then we try to make something from it. It's really fun." She put her banner down. Whew. That was over.

"Okay! My turn?" Yael asked before Maya even finished talking. "Thanks! I'm Yael, which I think I already told you out by the bus." She twisted a lock of hair up on her head and stuck a bobby pin in it in one smooth motion. "I'm from Boston and I'm eleven and I put camp really big on my banner because I've been going to camp since forever, just an all-girls one, like this one, so if anyone wants any advice or anything, just let me know. Like how to win color wars or do the Code of Silence—I'm really good at it. And I put a cat on here because I have a gray cat named Kevin. He's a Russian blue, and he sleeps under the covers with me. And I really, really, really miss him."

"Your cat's named *Kevin*?" Marisa asked.

"I like that name." Maya was surprised to hear her own voice. Maybe it had something to do with the way Yael's face looked when she talked about Kevin.

"Okay, great intros," Tamar broke in. "So, you already know that we're the Akko cabin. But I bet you don't know our cabin cheer yet. We do our cheers all the time here at Shalom—when we're walking to the dining hall or to the meadow for sports or while we're waiting to eat. The cabin that cheers the loudest gets to eat first."

There was a little ripple of excitement around the group.

Tamar went on. "So our cheer is 'A-K-K-O, Akko, Akko, *clap, clap,* let's go!'" Tamar's claps were so unexpected that they startled half the group into audible gasps.

"A-K-K-O, Akko, Akko, let's go!" Maya chanted along with everyone else.

"Come on!" Tamar said. "We're supposed to be *loud!*"

"A-K-K-O, Akko, Akko, let's go!" Maya shouted. She was a little self-conscious that the other cabins might be able to hear her through the screen windows.

"Good, that's loud enough," Tamar said. "Let's go over a few camp rules." She held up a grayish object that at first Maya thought was a piece of wood. It turned out to be an extremely dirty tube sock. "This is the Dirty Sock Award," Tamar said. "We're pretty strict here at Shalom about neatness, so we have cabin inspections every morning. The messiest cabin has to put this on a stand in the middle of the dining hall, and they have to clear tables after the meal!" She flipped the tube sock into the Dani's lap, and Dani caught it automatically.

"*Whoa*, it, like, stands up on its own." Dani balanced it on the floor in front her.

"Yep," Tamar said. "It's never been washed since Camp Shalom was founded fifty years ago. It's a special camp artifact. So, starting tomorrow morning, beds made, all dirty clothes in the laundry bags, everything else in the cubbies. Max will be by to inspect." She took a folded piece of paper from her shorts pocket and spread it on the floor in front of her. "Then we'll start our day's activities. Breakfast is at eight, and then we go to activities as a cabin. We usually have two activities per morning—like ropes course, nature education, outdoor cooking, kayaking—"

"Yeah!" Gracie broke in. "I love kayaking!"

Maya thought maybe she should reconsider her idea to rope herself to Gracie during the nuclear apocalypse.

Tamar smiled. "That's great. We have waterfront activities every day, so you'll have lots of time to practice. We have paddle-boarding too." She looked down at the paper. Maya's leg was going to sleep. She wiggled it around until the prickles were gone. "Then lunch is at noon, and then we have an hour of rest. Then another activity—swimming lessons, if we didn't have them in the morning, or something else, like the clay studio or painting. Then free time, when you can wander and hang out, then dinner at six. After dinner, there's some kind of evening program around the campfire, and then we have showers and lights out at nine thirty. Okay!" Tamar looked around them. "I know that's a lot to take in—you'll get used to it really fast, trust me."

"Also, what about color wars?" Yael broke in. She was sitting up very straight, her tan legs folded underneath her, lotus-style. Maya admired her swirly bun for the billionth time. "At my old camp, we always did color wars the last week—here's how it worked. So first you had a red team and a blue team—"

"*Um*, are we even doing that here?" Marisa asked.

"It's okay, Yael, thanks for explaining," Tamar said. "Yes, we have color wars but it's at the end of the summer. I was actually going to tell you guys about the *other* big event we've got coming up really soon: Akko is leading the first Shabbat. If you haven't been to camp before, a camp Shabbat is really special. We welcome Shabbat outside, in our amphitheater by the lake. And each cabin takes a turn leading service. We're first, so we'll spend this week getting ready. We'll choose some poems to read and then we'll rehearse—it's almost like putting on a performance."

"Oh!" Yael sat up even straighter. "Performing! Like, reading aloud. That's great! I *love* reading aloud! It's like so special." She looked around the group as if for confirmation. Dani gave her an uncertain smile.

So special? Maya never really thought about readings

being special. Mostly, they were just full of hard words. Leading Shabbat sounded like fun though, as long as there weren't too many people staring at her. She wasn't crazy about that, even though she'd had lots of practice in Speech and Debate at school.

Tamar looked at her watch. "Okay, guys, almost time for swimming tests! We'll get ready for the lake now. Get your suits on and bring your towels. You'll need your water sandals too," Tamar continued. She had a way of saying things that made you forget even the thought of protesting. They must teach them how to talk like that in the army.

Maya's heart fell into her sneakers. Swimming tests already! But the lake was so big. Wasn't there maybe a large puddle she could take her test in?

"Each of you will need to swim out to the floating dock and back," Tamar told them. "It's not that hard, but we do need to make sure you're strong swimmers. When we go on our sleepover at Snake Island in a couple weeks, there's going to be a lot of canoeing and swimming. You've got to pass the test to go on the sleepover, but don't worry. No camper's ever failed."

And that record is about to be broken, Maya thought.

Tamar got up, and everyone else climbed to their feet. "Put shorts over your suits because we'll go straight to lunch after."

Everyone scattered to their bunks. Maya could hear

her heart beating in her ears as she sorted through her duffel to find her blue-and-white striped bathing suit. She kept trying to swallow back the bad feeling that was rising in her throat but somehow her mouth felt too dry. It was important to act normal though, so she forced her fingers to keep pulling on her suit. Like a robot, she adjusted her straps and rooted out her towel. Dani dropped down wearing a bright-purple suit and holding a turquoise towel. Gracie had a navy-blue suit with "PCY Tigersharks" on the front, and Marisa was wearing a pilly green one that was all stretched out in the rear. She didn't seem to care though. Yael was already out the door in a perfect white tankini with little boy shorts.

Outside, girls were banging in and out of the other cabins. Already towels were draped over the porch railings. "HAH-hah-HAH, HAIFA!" Maya heard through the screens of the neighboring cabin. That was the one with Annie and Rachel. Wearing a yellow-and-black backpack, Tamar led them down another pine needle-covered path, away from the office and the dining hall. They passed through a scrubby area full of bushes with small white flowers, and then Maya could see the lake glinting through the trees. The water looked darker than it had on the bus. Maya kept walking—what else was she going to do?—but the worry was creeping up her throat. Mom called it "anxious heart."

She walked more and more slowly, until the group

pulled ahead. No one noticed. Gracie was talking to Marisa, and Yael was walking alone, her head down. Then Dani turned around and came back down the path toward her. "What are you doing back here? Are you okay?"

Maya nodded. She didn't trust her voice.

Dani fell into step beside her and narrowed her eyes. "You don't look okay. What's wrong?"

"I—I have a secret," Maya whispered.

"What?" Dani bent over.

Maya's mouth was so dry, it hurt to swallow. "I'm afraid to swim." There. She'd said it. She still had an anxious heart though.

"In the lake or in any water?" Dani asked.

"Any water." Maya watched her sneakers mash the thick layer of pine needles covering the path.

"Why? Do you know how to swim?"

"Yeah, I can swim a little." Maya made herself keep talking. "I, *um*, I had a bad experience at day camp last summer." Quickly, she explained what happened with Miles and the pool. It was weird to say the whole story out loud. It made it seem real all over again.

Dani was listening with her mouth open. "Wow, that's so scary. How did you get out?"

"A lifeguard saw what was happening and jumped in. She saved me. I coughed up what felt like a gallon of water. I felt like I would never catch my breath again."

34

"Wow. I never saw a lifeguard actually save someone," Dani said.

"I know, me neither." Maya took a deep breath. Her anxious heart felt better. "Ever since then, I just feel panic when I have to get in the water. I'm going to fail the swim test. I know it."

"No! You won't! You can do this!" Dani said with an encouraging smile.

"How?" Maya asked miserably. "But here's the thing I'm really worried about. It's not even the swim test. I mean it is. But how can I go on the Snake Island sleepover if I don't pass? They'll have to leave me here alone. Or maybe they'll send me home."

"No!" Dani patted her back. "We'll figure something out. I'll help you."

Ahead of them, the path sloped downward, then widened out onto a small, sandy beach. The Akkos spread out, investigating the paddleboards lined up in a rack at one end. Yellow and orange kayaks were overturned nearby, and the rows of life jackets and oars stood like racks of armor. Out in the dark water, a big wooden float bobbed gently. To Maya, it looked as far away as Mexico. Maya heard a sudden scream and splash, and she whipped around, ready to find the drowning victim. Instead, she saw a figure fly out of a huge green tube and splash into the lake.

"That's the Green Monster," Tamar explained. "It's

our homemade water slide. Starts in the woods. To get there, you have to climb up some wooden stairs. It goes crazy fast, and it shoots you down here."

"*Oooh*, awesome!" Gracie said. "When can we do it? Now? Can we?"

A counselor with two long brown braids and a red tank suit interrupted the excitement. "Okay! Welcome to the waterfront! I'm Leah, the swimming counselor, and you all need swim tests. Let's get you started so you can have fun in the water this summer."

CHAPTER 3

"Go, Dani!" Marisa shouted fifteen minutes later. The other Akkos were lined up on the sandy beach, shivering, dripping, and clutching towels around their shoulders. Each of them had breezed through the swim tests like they were part dolphin. Over and over, Maya watched their sleek arms and legs cutting through the water, touching the wood raft, and gliding back again.

Dani waded in from the lake, grinning. Gracie threw a red towel at her that landed on her head. "Yeah, girl! Snake Island!"

"Okay, Maya, you're next!" Leah called from her position knee-high in the water. Maya thought there was a good chance she'd pass out. Maybe she *could* pass out— that way she wouldn't have to take the swim test.

"Ready?" the counselor smiled at her. "Don't worry— this is simple. Just a formality."

Maya barely heard her. She shuffled forward. The lake seemed huge, with no end to it. The smell of mud and reeds rose up around her as she stepped in. Her feet sank into the squishy mud. She waded, arms out, as the water crept up to her knees, then her waist, then her ribs.

Suddenly, she stopped. "Sorry. Can I do this later?"

Leah waded up beside her, with Tamar. "Sorry, but this is when the swim tests are. You want to have free swim this afternoon, right? We're going to take the kayaks out."

"Ah . . ." Maya glanced back at the knot of girls standing on the narrow strip of beach. It looked like the Haifas were there now, too, along with the Akkos. She could see Rachel's curly head. Dani caught her eye and gave an encouraging thumbs-up. "I do want to swim." Biggest lie in the world. "It's just that, *um* . . ." Her cheeks were growing hot.

"What's wrong, Maya?" Tamar asked.

She probably never wimped out on swim tests in the Israeli army. "I'm not super good at swimming," Maya mumbled.

Tamar and Leah looked at each other. "It's okay," Tamar said gently. "You don't have to go on the overnight. The seven-year-olds will be here and you can stay with them and their counselors."

Great.

"Well, maybe I can just sit out *today*," Maya tried.

"You really need to at least give it a shot," Tamar said. "There are no quitters in Akko."

"Maybe I can be the first?" Maya gave them a weak smile, but Tamar steered Maya a few steps deeper into the water.

"Just show us what you can do," Tamar said.

Maya felt her whole body tighten.

"Come on," Leah said. "I'll be right here."

Maya thought maybe she would cry. Instead, she took another step. And another step. She glanced over her shoulder. Everyone was staring. The Haifas and Gracie, Yael, Marisa, and Dani were sitting down on the sand now, watching like they were at the movies. She half expected them to have tubs of popcorn.

Another step. The lake water spread around her. It seemed as big as an ocean. An ocean to swallow her up. How could she lift her feet up and swim? What if the bottom dropped away, and there were huge fish swimming and one of them brushed her leg? With that same awful feeling Maya had at the pool, she saw herself choking in the water. She shivered. The water was so cold. She longed for the dry, rough comfort of her towel.

Maya glanced at Leah and Tamar. They were both watching her, smiling encouragingly. She took another step. Something soft moved under her foot, and she let out a squeak. An eel? Were there eels in here? She looked down at her white legs disappearing into the dark water and willed them to move. She reached forward and lifted her feet.

"You can do it, Maya!" a faint voice called from the beach. No. No, she could not.

She scrabbled frantically for the bottom. "I can't!" she burst out. "Okay? I can't! I'm no good at swimming." She couldn't tell them about the fear that was crowding up from her stomach, pushing behind her teeth, filling every part of her. She couldn't tell a former member of the Israeli army she was scared of water. She tried to splash back to the beach but ran into Tamar's hard abdomen. Her counselor caught her by the shoulders.

"Okay, okay," Tamar said. "So, we've got some work to do. But we'll get there! You got your feet up—that was good! You'll make the raft by the end of the summer, I promise!"

Yeah, that'll never happen, Maya thought as she picked her way back to the beach. "You'll get it next time," Dani said as Maya sank down on the warm, dank sand. The other Akkos clustered around, with the Haifas behind them. Rachel leaned over and whispered something to one of the others, who giggled. Were they making fun of her?

"So, you can't swim?" Rachel asked. She had one of those pretend-confused looks on her face. She was wearing a swimsuit with a skirt bottom, like the one Maya's mom had.

Dani put her arm around Maya's shoulders and scowled at Rachel. "She can swim!"

Marisa pressed in beside them. "I hate tests too," she confessed. "At school, I get stomachaches. Then I have to go to the bathroom, and I have this imaginary donkey named Hun-Hun, who I pretend is there with me, and I pet him—I mean, not really, because he's imaginary— and then I feel a little better, and I go back to class."

There was a little pause.

"Ah yeah," Gracie said. "Anyway, I didn't learn to dive until last year, and it was really, really hard."

"Me neither!" Yael offered. "I just jumped off the high dive *once* at the swim club, but I got scared halfway through and ended up doing a belly flop. It really hurt! And everyone saw."

Maya offered them a watery smile. She felt a tiny bit better. It felt good to have the support, even if she'd just met these girls.

They wrapped up in their towels and pulled their shorts on over damp suits. As they walked up the sandy path from the lake, Dani fell in beside Maya. "Did you tell them, you know, about what you told me?"

Maya shook her head. "It's too embarrassing."

"I don't think it's embarrassing," Dani said. She

linked her arm with Maya's. "Everyone's afraid of something. I'm still kind of scared of taking out the garbage."

Maya laughed. "What's scary about garbage?"

"It's not the garbage that's scary—it's just that garbage cans are out behind our garage, and it's really dark out there. And what if there are rats, like, scuttling around, and when I'm putting the cans back, one of them jumps up and bites into my arm?"

A little shiver passed through Maya as she pictured the black night, the bushes crowding near the garage, Dani struggling to take off the heavy can lid and then lifting the bag, but before she could put in it, a disgusting rat tail . . .

"Okay, yeah, I take it back," Maya said. "Garbage *is* terrifying."

Up ahead, they could see that Tamar had stopped at a clearing in the pine trees. In the middle, a large fire circle was ringed with stones. "This is campfire cooking, everyone," Tamar said. "We'll make our lunch here once a week, beginning today. Now, Marisa and Yael, grab those grates and set them up on the stands in the middle of the fire ring."

"*Ew*, they're all sticky!" Yael grimaced, wiping her fingers on her white shorts. Maya was a tiny bit glad to see the greasy streaks they left. Who wears white at an outdoor camp?

At Tamar's direction, the girls scattered, collecting dry sticks and small branches. Then Tamar demonstrated how to build a log cabin fire. "The tinder goes in the middle, then then the kindling is heaped loosely around it. The logs surround it in a square." Her tanned hands moved with authority.

Dani leaned over to Maya. "Israeli army," she whispered.

Maya nodded. They probably built fires all the time out there in the desert on night patrol.

Once the fire was going, the girls wrapped packets of corn, sliced peppers, and turkey dogs in foil. Maya tried to balance hers on the grate, but it kept slipping through the bars. "I think mine's the wrong shape," she said.

"Oh, you just need to make it more square." Gracie gave the foil pack an authoritative squeeze.

"Now that everyone's all set cooking, I want to tell you guys a little more about our Snake Island sleepover in a couple of weeks," Tamar said. Her own foil packet was expertly shaped.

"How long do we go?" Marisa asked.

"Marisa, your food's on fire." Tamar pointed at a flaming pepper sticking out of her packet. Without skipping a beat, she answered the question. "We'll be on the island for four nights. We'll take camp canoes out— it's a two-hour trip—and we bring all our own supplies. Tents, food, tarps, even water. Then we'll spend four days exploring the island, swimming, and learning all about wilderness survival."

"Survival?" Marisa asked as she tried to blow out her burning lunch. Her eyes were wide. "Like we have to *survive* out there?"

"If the Wareloch doesn't get us, we'll survive," Tamar said, lowering her voice and leaning in. The others automatically leaned in too. "No one knows what he looks like, but he's haunted Snake Island for a hundred years. Other campers say they've heard him scratching on the outside of their tents at night." She burst into maniacal laughter. No one could tell if she was kidding or not. Maya was too old to believe in ghosts, but something about Tamar's face sent a shiver up her spine. "Anyway, Snake Island is a Camp Shalom tradition. Every camper over nine has gone out there since the very first season of camp." She looked at her watch. "Now we've got to get cleaned up and get ready for opening ceremony down at the amphitheater."

The girls smothered the fire and put their trash in the paper bag Tamar had brought. Maya's stomach was so heavy. It wasn't just the turkey dog. It was Tamar's last words. *Every camper over nine has gone out there since the very first season of camp.* If she didn't pass the swim test, she'd be the first one. Ever.

At the chadar ochel entrance with the gum tree, Tamar led them inside. "We just have to make a quick stop." She opened a storage closet near the kitchen and gathered up some items. "These are all the things we'll need to lead Shabbat at the end of the week." She handed out two short white candles and an embroidered challah cover. Then she unlocked a dented green metal box. Everyone crowded around to see.

Inside, a silver kiddush cup and two silver candlesticks rested on a bed of worn red velvet. "These are very special to the camp," Tamar said. "Obviously, they're silver, so they're valuable. But more than that, these are our founder's own kiddush cup and candlesticks. He was the grandfather of our director, Max. He brought them from Europe himself when his family immigrated here." Carefully, she closed and locked the box again. "They stay in here until Shabbat." She put the box back on the shelf and took down a thick blue plastic goblet and two cheap tin candlesticks. Maya could tell they were the same kind Mom kept at home for when the power went out. "The camp keeps these for us to practice with," Tamar said. She handed the goblet to Maya and the candlesticks to Dani. "We don't want the silver sitting around in the cabin. We'll use the real stuff when we actually lead Shabbat."

They all shuffled out, and Tamar called, "Everyone just wait here. I have to return the keys." She carefully locked the storage cabinet and disappeared past a wall phone, a fire extinguisher, and a sculpture of a tree down a short hallway that led from the mess hall. Everyone else was talking, but by craning her head, Maya could see her disappear into a door marked "Max Samson – Director." They must keep the keys in there.

She'd only been at Camp Shalom for half a day, but when they pushed open the screen door to the cabin, it almost felt like they were coming home. Maya's sleeping bag and heart pillow looked very cozy, waiting for her on her bunk. The dappled light from the trees danced a pattern on the floor. Maybe this would be a nice place to spend the next seven weeks.

Tamar raised the lid of the footlocker at the end of her bed. "This is where we'll keep the Shabbat things until we need them," she said, nestling the plastic cup and candlesticks, the candles, and the challah cover in among some spare sheets. She closed the lid and latched it. "Okay! Let's get ready for opening ceremony. This is where we all officially meet as a camp. We'll sing some camp songs, the counselors do a skit, and Max will go over camp rules, that sort of thing. But all the cabins get dressed up in their own special outfits. So . . ." She went over to a top cubby and pulled out a bag Maya hadn't noticed before. She started pulling stuff out. Pots of yellow face paint, glow bracelets, and a packet of yellow bandannas fell onto her sleeping bag. "Our color is yellow, so we'll all paint out faces, tie our hair up . . . Have at it, Akkos!"

"*Oooh*, fun!" Dani said. Everyone took a bandanna, and for the next half hour the cabin was full of chatter, dropped hairbrushes, and face painting. By the time Tamar told them it was time to go, they were ready—hair in two matching braids, Tamar's bandannas on their heads, and two streaks of yellow face paint on their cheeks.

"We look great," Dani said. She draped one arm over Maya's shoulder and one over Yael's. The others pressed in, forming a circle with their arms around each other's backs. *It felt like a hug*, Maya thought.

"A-K-K-O!" they all chanted. "Akko, Akko, let's go!" Their voices vibrated together. Maya knew she had a huge grin on her face. It felt good to be on a team, all of them together. She was glad her face was painted the same way as the others and they were wearing the same bandannas. She never thought she'd care about that until this moment, but guess what? She did.

They broke their circle and crowded out, letting the screen door slam behind them and leaving the cabin empty and silent again.

CHAPTER 4

Everywhere, Maya could see girls streaming out of the cabins, wearing their matching T-shirts—green, yellow, red, purple, black—shockingly bright against the greens and browns of the trees and grass and dirt. Everyone had matching hair too—braids like theirs, or buns or one braid or French braids—but no one had face paint like the Akkos. As the groups joined together on the gravel path and started down toward the lake, the cabin cheers rose up, sounding small in the open air. Maya yelled the Akko chant as loud as she could. The sun was setting, and the sky was painted soft gray and rose. The good scent of pine needles and earth hung in the still evening air. Maya didn't think she'd ever been this happy before.

The amphitheater was an open spot facing the lake, with wooden benches in tiers facing a big wooden platform stage. Some kind of reddish mulch covered the ground. Behind the stage, the lake rippled, with the setting sun cutting a pink and gold path across the water.

When everyone was sitting with their cabin, Max bounded onto the stage. He was wearing a Camp Shalom rainbow T-shirt and holding a microphone. "Hello, Camp Shalom!" he shouted. Everyone let out a huge scream, cheering. *It was like being at a concert*, Maya thought, even though she'd never been to a concert. *But this must be what it was like.*

Another counselor with a green bandanna around his curly hair, and a guitar, ran onto the stage beside Max. A girl with a guitar and a guy with a drum followed. They immediately swung into a song:

Boom, boom, ain't it great to be crazy!
Boom, boom, ain't it great to be crazy!
Silly and crazy all day long,
Boom, boom, ain't it great to be crazy!

Everyone was clapping, and some kids like Gracie were singing along, but then the bandanna song leader pointed at everyone and shouted, "Repeat after me! One line at a time! *A horse and a flea and three blind mice!*"

"A horse and a flea and three blind mice!" Maya sang back, her voice blending with all the others around her.

"Sat on a curbstone shooting dice!"

"Sat on a curbstone shooting dice!" they sang.

Maya looked around as she sang, at the mass of other singing girls—Dani on one side of her and Yael on the other, and the pine trees watching them in the gathering dark. *I'm here. I'm really doing it. I'm at camp.* Home might as well have been on the moon, for how close it felt. At this moment, singing together, Camp Shalom felt like home.

After the song, Max took the mic again. "These are our song leaders, Damien, Lucas, and Elise—you're going to be seeing a lot of them! They play at lunch and dinner, every day during campfire song time, and during Shabbat. Speaking of Shabbat, I want to introduce our first cabin Shabbat leaders—the Akkos!"

Everyone turned around and stared and cheered. "Come on, stand up!" Tamar urged, and Maya popped up and down as fast as she could. Yael didn't get up at all until Marisa tugged her arm.

"And now, just a few camp rules I want to go over," Max went on. "No one is to be in the cabins during activity time. No food in the cabins—unless you want a raccoon rummaging through your stuff."

Over the laughter, Max went on. "Reminder that Camp Shalom is a phone-free camp! That means no cell phones, no smart watches, nothing but real face-to-face communication! There is a phone in the hallway outside my office, but it is strictly off-limits unless you have a counselor with you and it's an emergency."

Some girls were being really noisy behind them. Maya turned around and saw a group of older girls—

maybe thirteen—at the back, giggling about something. One girl, tall, red-faced, and wearing what looked like a pith helmet, was doing an imitation of something—Max, Maya realized after a minute. She was holding a pretend mic up to her mouth and bobbing around, while the rest of her bunk watched with amusement. Dani turned around and saw them, too, and made a face. "Annoying," she whispered, and Maya nodded. She could tell the pith helmet girl was the type who always wore some goofy outfit and sat in the back of the classroom making loud jokes just to get people to look at her. It wasn't very nice of her to make fun of Max. He was just explaining the rules. And she was ruining all the magic of the ceremony.

Maya started to turn around, only to spot Rachel, sitting with Annie and the other Haifas a few rows over. Rachel was practically the polar opposite of the pith helmet girl. She was sitting perfectly still with her hands folded in her lap, as if she were in synagogue, and her eyes fixed on Max. All right, all right. She was obviously perfect. Maya mentally rolled her eyes and trained her attention on the platform again.

"And now," Max was saying. "We are going to officially open our summer camping season. Get to your feet, campers!"

The song leader with the drum started beating it again, with big, rapid thumps that pounded in Maya's chest. "Stand up!" Tamar motioned them. As they stood,

Yael suddenly wiggled in beside them; her face was red and her hair was disheveled, as if she'd been running.

"Yael, you need to ask permission to go to the bathroom," Tamar said. "I have to keep track of you guys."

"Sorry! I'm sorry!" Yael said. "I really had to go." Her eyes were darting from one Akko to the next. "I'll ask next time. Sorry, Tamar!"

"Okay, calm down, it's not a big deal," Tamar said. "Just remember for the future, okay?"

"As the sun drops over the horizon," Max said, "we light our first bonfire of the camping season. Its light will burn after the heat and light of the sun have left us. It is the same light that is within all Camp Shalom campers."

Gracie sniffled, and Maya realized she was crying. Tears started up in her own eyes immediately, and then Dani was crying too. They draped their arms around each other's shoulders and swayed back and forth.

"The camper chosen to light the opening bonfire is here for her last summer at Shalom. She represents both beginning and ending."

A tall girl with long blonde hair joined Max as he walked over to a circle of stones set well away from the platform. Maya hadn't noticed the pile of sticks and split logs there before. Max handed the girl a long match. The sun was dropping lower and lower over the lake. The whole camp was watching. Maya couldn't take her eyes from the tiny slice of red hovering over the lake horizon. Everyone else was watching, too, their bodies absolutely still. The silence was broken only by sniffles. The sun dropped a little lower and then a little lower. Then it slid slowly, slowly behind the lake. It was gone. Max nodded to the girl, and she struck the long match and touched it to the inner part of the pile.

A massive exhale moved through the campers, and rich chords on the guitars floated out over them as the song leaders sang,

"We will love, we will learn,

Let us teach now those in turn,

Others follow the paths we've trod,

We'll light the flame for those to come."

Maya's throat was all achy, but it felt good. How could summer camp only be seven weeks? Already, she couldn't bear to think of leaving. The flames climbed higher and higher as everyone joined in the simple song. Maya glanced down at her fellow Akkos. They looked so beautiful and otherworldly with their painted faces glowing in the orange light from the fire.

Then Tamar slipped out of their row, and Maya realized all the counselors were threading their way down toward the bonfire. They clustered together in front of the campers, and the fire crackled and spit behind them, sending spark showers up into the dark-gray sky.

"Camp Shalom is the best!" all the counselors shouted together. "We don't know about the rest!"

"Camp Shalom is the best! We don't know about the rest!" Maya shouted back, as loud as she could, until she could feel the words scraping against the inside of her throat. They were all Camp Shalomers together. Except, she realized, the older cabin with the pith helmet girl. They weren't Camp Shalomers together. Because they were gone. Only a bare section of bench showed where they had been.

"Hey." She nudged Dani. "Those girls are gone."

Dani twisted around to look. "Really? Weird. Where'd they go?"

"Camp Shalom is the best!" everyone was cheering again, and Maya chimed in.

Then the ceremony was over, and they were all shuffling out, scuffing their feet through the red mulch.

"That was intense," Dani said.

"So intense," Maya agreed, trying to navigate her way through the narrow board seats. They were all squashed together in the traffic jam. "I didn't know I was going to cry!"

"I always cry," Gracie volunteered from behind them. "Every year! I just love it so much."

"*Ooowww!*" Someone in front of Maya stopped suddenly. It was Rachel, the girl with the grumpy face.

Annie was beside her. Rachel twisted around. Her forehead was all knotted up above her glasses.

"You stepped on my heel," she said to Maya.

"Sorry." Maya offered her a little suck-up smile. She hated making people mad. Rachel-types always sniffed her out.

"It was an accident," Annie told Rachel. "Hi, Maya!"

"Hi! Bye!" Maya called over her shoulder as the crowd of girls swept her along. They filtered up the path with the others, the pine needles crunching under their feet. The sky was dark now, and through the dark trunks of the pine trees, Maya could see the moon rising. She lifted her face to the night breeze. It smelled different from at home. Like earth and leaves and lake water.

Tamar clicked on a big flashlight. The other counselors had flashlights, too, and everywhere on the paths the lights bobbed, surrounded by dark figures. The sound of giggling and talking rose and filtered into the branches overhead. Maya felt a sudden lift of happiness and linked her arm with Dani's. The swim test was over, for better or worse. She could do this camp thing. Maybe she'd figure out her swimming problem.

She bounded up the steps to the cabin along with everyone else. "Shower time!" Tamar announced. "Everyone get your towels and bathrobes—" She stopped suddenly.

"What is it?" Yael asked.

Tamar shook her head. "The door's open. I always latch it to keep animals out." She stepped inside. The rest of the girls followed. Immediately, Maya saw the footlocker, pushed askew, with the latch undone. Everyone else saw it too.

Tamar stepped over to the trunk. She lifted the lid. The girls crowded behind her, peering in. Then Dani gasped. The practice kiddush cup, candlesticks, candles, and challah cover were gone.

CHAPTER 5

Everyone watched as Tamar pawed through the trunk, pulling out spare sheets and pillowcases. Finally, she straightened up. "Girls, did one of you move these things?"

"No! No!" Everyone shook their heads.

"We haven't been up here since we went down to the lake," Dani said.

Maya scraped the bottom of her bare foot against her calf. Camp was definitely going to be dirty—already there was mulch on the floor of the cabin.

"Maybe an animal took them." Yael was speaking very fast. Her big blue eyes were wide. "Guys! Listen! I bet it was a racoon. They can open anything—like at home, they even open this latch we have on our poolhouse, and they get in there, and one time, my brother left out a bag of Doritos, and they ate the whole thing."

Tamar slowly lowered the lid. "I don't know about that. All I know is that these things are gone." She fixed the Akkos with a direct gaze. "They didn't vaporize out of the trunk. Someone or something took them. And we have to find them. If we don't, we'll have to practice with something else. Maybe another bunk is pranking us."

Gracie squealed. "OMG, prank wars!" She rushed over to her bunk and started rummaging in her duffel bag. "Listen you guys, I have shaving cream. What you do is, you get a really old banana and you smash it up, then you get a sock, cut a hole in the end—"

"I can't believe someone would just come in here and steal our stuff," Marisa said. She was standing with her hands on her hips. "Just march right in here! I don't care if it's a prank or what. That's just not right. Who even does that?"

"The stuff is *stolen*?" Maya asked. She peered over Tamar's shoulder into the trunk. Rumpled sheets, some stray bits of clothing—and that was all.

"Stolen?" Yael echoed. "Whoa, what?"

"Wait you guys, I bet it's Eilat—they have this tradition of pranks, and last year, they hung all these gross pond weeds from the top of the cabin door, and when we opened it in the morning, we all ran right into them!" Gracie jumped up on her lower bunk in excitement. "We've got to get them back!"

"All right, settle down," Tamar raised her voice. "Whatever's happened, we're not going to solve it right now. Get your towels, shower shoes, caddies, and bathrobes. We've only got fifteen minutes for showers."

The shower house was damp and noisy. Each stall had a shower curtain across it and a pair of flip-flopped feet underneath. Three little girls were brushing their teeth at the row of sinks, supervised by their counselor, and a girl with long red hair was trying to dry it under the hand dryer mounted to the wall. Maya clutched her bathrobe around her. She didn't really want to take off all her clothes in this mossy-smelling cinderblock room, but she also felt extremely grungy. She was dying to wash off the lake smell.

But before she could contemplate the shower any further, Dani grabbed her arm and steered her toward two empty sinks way down at the end. "Here, look like you're brushing your teeth," she muttered. She dug a twisted tube of toothpaste out of her caddy.

Maya found her purple toothbrush case and the new toothpaste Mom had packed—a little stab of homesickness pricked her in the heart when she thought of Mom's hands putting it in her caddy as they sat packing on the carpeted floor of the attic.

"A real mystery!" Dani said around her toothpaste. Her face was all lit up. "Right here at camp! Maya, we have to find the Shabbat stuff—just like Sherlock Holmes!" She spat and rinsed from a little travel cup. "We'll use our powers of deduction!"

"But what if it was just a prank?" Maya bared her foamy teeth in the mirror. "Gracie said that other bunk does a lot of pranks."

"I mean, maybe." Dani capped her toothpaste. "But what if it's not just a prank? What if it's something more sinister? We should really follow the clues." Her dark eyes were wide.

"Right," Maya said. "We'll follow the clues." She felt a thrill of excitement zing through her. "But if it's not a prank, then what's going on, do you think? Is it some kind of weird accident? Or did someone take our things on purpose?" She followed Dani to the shower stalls. Marisa was in one, judging by the black slides beneath the curtain. Gracie was combing her wet hair in front of the mirror. Yael was sitting on a bench with her leg up, filing her toenails.

Dani paused in front of the shower stalls. "We'll have to make a list of possibilities—how could the items have gone missing? Accident? Misunderstanding? Or—do we have a *thief*?"

The word zinged like it had an electric charge. Maya and Dani stared at each other. "A thief!" Maya said. "What?" She clutched the mildew-spotted shower curtain beside her.

"But wait," Dani said. "Never assume—that's what Holmes always says. We'll have to investigate." She whisked into the shower, and a second later Maya heard the rush of water as she pulled the chain. She stepped more slowly into her own stall, taking care not to let her bathrobe or towel drop on the soaking wet, slightly slimy concrete floor. She let the hot water run down over her and spray on her face. A thief. Was it? Could it be?

Maya lay in her bunk after lights-out, her head cradled on her hand, looking out the screened window near her face and thinking. It had only been day one of camp and already her mind was stuffed. The lake, the candlesticks and kiddush cup, the bonfire, Rachel's scowling face, Dani's friendly face, Tamar's strong arms, the voices rising from the amphitheater all swirled in her head, until she finally fell asleep.

CHAPTER 6

"Okay, guys, team meeting." Everyone gathered around Dani outside the dining hall. She had an intense expression. Maya crowded in. Dani pulled out her copy of *The Hound of the Baskervilles* and opened the front cover. The title page was covered with tiny notes in pencil.

"Let me lay it out for you." Dani read from her notes. "Someone or something has, obviously, absconded with our Shabbat stuff."

Marisa raised her hand. "What's *absconded* mean?"

"It means taken, so listen." She ticked off the items. "Maya and I have concluded that we could have either one, a misunderstanding; two, a prank; or three, a thief!"

"*Eek!*" Gracie squealed. "A thief!"

"But wait, we don't know that," Yael broke in. Her

eyes darted from one Akko to another. "What about an animal? You didn't say that, Dani."

"Oh, right, animal." Dani scribbled in her book briefly. "So, breakfast is a great chance to do some investigating. Is anyone acting suspicious? Is anyone watching *us*? If it was a prank, they'll want to see how *we're* reacting. So act normal."

"Okay! Normal! Got it!" Marisa gritted her teeth and grinned at the same time.

"Not like that," Maya told her. "Show less teeth."

"Like this?" Marisa lifted her top lip so she looked like a dog growling.

"*Um*, kind of." Maya followed the others into the big, steamy, noisy, cavernous dining hall that smelled like pancakes and syrup this morning. Big tables on wheels extended from end to end, and there was a machine on the wall where you could get milk or orange juice. By the kitchen window a big stack of greenish trays and brownish plastic plates sat waiting on the metal rails.

Maya's stomach gurgled loudly. Food first, investigation later. She took a plate, and handed it to the smiling, bearded guy behind the window. He flopped three pancakes onto it from an enormous pan, then added two kosher sausage links and handed it back. A huge bowl of orange slices sat at the end of the rails.

Maya took a few and joined the rest of the cabin at the Akkos' spot.

"Do you see anything weird?" Dani muttered when she sat down.

Maya looked around. Campers sat packed on the benches, eating, talking, shoving pitchers of juice back and forth across the table to each other. She spotted the pith helmet girl and the Eilat group. "Guys," she said, leaning in. "What about them? They have a history of pranks, remember? Who's that one wearing the helmet?"

"Cori," Gracie answered. "That's her signature."

"Oh yeah!" Yael said immediately. "Are they acting suspicious, do you think? I can go eavesdrop; I'm all done." Her plate was clean except for one orange slice.

"Aren't you hungry?" Gracie asked.

Yael smiled but somehow, it looked forced. "No! Not this morning! I never eat a big breakfast." Her happy voice sounded forced, too. She jumped up. Everyone watched as she casually strolled by the Eilat table toward the milk machine. They were subdued this morning. The pith helmet girl was eating with her helmet over her eyes, hunched over her cereal bowl.

Yael ostentatiously filled a small glass with milk, then slowly strolled back to the Akkos, past the Eilats again.

"Well?" Dani asked after she sat down. "Anything?"

"They were talking about the ropes course," Yael said. "That's it."

Dani slumped in her seat. "Boo."

"Hi."

Everyone looked up. Grumpy Rachel stood by their table, holding a notebook and a pen. Maya noticed that her T-shirt was tucked into her shorts, like a mom's. "I'm helping with the *Camp Shalom News*," she said. "Do you guys have anything to report? I'm asking all the cabins."

"Oh good!" Tamar said. "Guys, this is our camp newspaper. It comes out once a week."

"*Do* we have something?" Dani jumped up and leaned her hands on the table. "*Do* we? Yes, actually we do." She paused dramatically. "There's been a disappearance."

Maya watched Rachel's face. She was rewarded only with that puckered-eyebrow scowl from the bus.

"What?" Rachel said. "What are you talking about?"

Everyone started talking at once, and by the time Rachel left their table, her notebook had the text for an ad that read, "Missing: Special items have gone missing from the Akko cabin. Please return or offer any tips as to their location. Reward!" They'd decided Dani would weave an extra-good friendship bracelet for anyone who could give a tip. The paper would be out in two days.

"Well, what about an animal, like Yael said?" Maya offered as everyone slowly got up from the table. Her own stomach felt extremely full. It was good that swimming wasn't until the afternoon. She'd definitely sink with all those pancakes in her.

Everyone stood around by the gum tree. Marisa took a wad of bright blue out of her mouth and stuck it on a bare spot on the trunk. "*Hmm*, yesss. . ." Dani stroked her chin with a thoughtful finger. Maya could almost see the imaginary beard. "We'll have to consult an animal expert."

"Who? We don't know anyone—we just got here."

"I know what to do," Dani said. "Gracie, who's the nature counselor here?"

"I guess Joel." She sounded unsure. "He's really just the groundskeeper."

"Tamar, can we go see him? Just for one minute." Dani clasped her hands together in front of her chest.

Tamar smiled. "Fine. But just you and Maya, and only for a minute because we're going to basketball. Go past the meadow and look for the nature shack. You'll know it's the nature shack because there's a sign above the door that says 'Nature Shack.'"

"That must be Israeli army humor," Maya said to Dani as they wound their way up the path back toward the office and headed for the meadow.

CHAPTER 7

Even though breakfast had just finished, the camp was already buzzing with kids and counselors everywhere. Maya could just see the colorful helmets of kids lining up for the ropes course, which swung up above their heads. Other groups were passing them on the path, going down to the lake for tubing. The gaga pit was already full, with kids yelling as they swatted the ball back and forth in the dust. The scent of pine was everywhere, the cicadas were singing in the trees, and the blue sky arched over everything.

The noises faded behind them though, as they hiked through the mowed path that cut through the meadow, past the art shack with its bowls of tie-dye standing ready, and on to the nature shack, which stood like a little outpost at the very end of the meadow.

Inside, they found a guy with red hair lowering a live mouse into the corn snake cage.

"Best not to look for a few minutes," Joel said, brushing off his hands.

Maya winced and looked away. Snakes needed to eat, too, but she didn't want to see it happen.

"What's up, girls?" Joel asked.

"We have a mystery in the Akko cabin," Dani said. "And we need your expertise." Quickly she explained what they'd found—or *not* found—in the cabin. "So, do you think an animal like a raccoon could have gotten in and taken the stuff?"

Joel shook his head. "Nope, girls. Raccoons are really good at undoing latches, and they're smart, but they tend to go for food only. A set of plastic candleholders and a cup wouldn't excite them enough to open a box. Besides, they're just not strong enough to lift a heavy lid. Most importantly, though, they're nocturnal. They never go out in the daytime unless they're sick."

Maya and Dani looked at each other. "I guess that crosses racoons off our list," Maya said.

"Possum?" Dani asked Joel.

"Nope. Also nocturnal. And too small."

"Umm, bear?"

"None around here. You need to drive like eight hours north for bears. To be honest, there aren't too many large mammals around here that can undo a latch—none, actually. We've just got deer and coyotes, and they're terrible at latches."

The girls looked at each other and nodded.

"Okay!" Maya said. "Thanks, Joel."

They cut through the large meadow back toward the mess hall. The morning sun was growing hot, and the grass was already dry. Maya sneezed twice. "Sorry, allergies."

"So, it wasn't an animal," Dani said. "And it wasn't the wind or something. I just thought of that."

"*Um*, yeah, I don't think the wind can lift the lid of a trunk."

Dani narrowed her eyes. "So. That only leaves a person."

"Right," Maya agreed. "He or she took the Shabbat stuff."

"Probably she. There's like two guys at this camp and we already talked to one," Maya pointed out.

"Right, good point. She."

"Now, listen." Dani stopped. She drew Holmes out of her pocket and held it like a talisman. "Obviously, someone could be pranking us. Or it's, like, a misunderstanding."

"Like maybe she thought the stuff was in the wrong place and she was supposed to put it back?" Maya asked. "That would be extremely weird."

"Right," Dani said. "Tamar put the stuff in there and

she said, 'it'll be safe in here,' and she closed the lid. Hard not to understand, right?"

Maya nodded and slapped a mosquito on the side of her neck. "I see what you're getting at. A person took the stuff. And that person must have done it on purpose. Either as a joke or *not* as a joke."

"Yep. A thief."

"Thief. Wow." Maya and Dani stopped walking and stared at each other with wide eyes. "We have a thief in our midst!" Maya said.

"Whether it's a prank or not, it's up to us to investigate," Dani said. "Just like Holmes and Watson would do."

During rest time, everyone was sacked out on their bunks. Tamar was at the counselor room; Gracie was listening to an old-school CD player with headphones; Marisa was dreamily weaving a friendship bracelet taped to her toe; and Yael was holding a book in front of her face. She didn't seem to be turning the pages though. It was the perfect time to bring the others up to date. "Hey, guys, listen," Maya said. "We talked to Joel the groundskeeper earlier." Quickly, she filled everyone in on the nature shack conversation.

"We have to catch the thief!" Yael bounced up off her bunk so hard Maya thought she might smack her head on the wall. "What if she strikes again? None of us is safe."

"Calm down, Yael. It's not a murderer," Marisa

called from her bunk. "I want to know why. Why would someone take our Shabbat stuff, even for a prank? It's not even valuable. Just a bunch of plastic."

Yael arranged herself cross-legged on her bed and hugged a big pillow. "Well, it's obvious, right? We can't lead Shabbat without all the stuff! We won't be able to practice—it just wouldn't be fair. It was—Shabbat sabotage!" she said dramatically.

"Wow," Dani said. Everyone digested that thought for a moment. *Why* in the world would anyone want to sabotage Shabbat? Of all the pranks there were to pull in the world, why this?

"Well, whatever their motives, we can't just sit back and let this happen. We're the Shabbat leaders! How does it look if everything gets stolen under our watch? We have to get it back," Maya said. "And to do that, we have to catch the thief." She thought of the pith helmet girl, Cori, sneaking into the cabin. Something just wasn't adding up. It seemed too . . . stealthy for Cori. Would that really be her style?

"Totally!" Dani agreed.

"Let's set a trap," Gracie suggested. "Like with bait. I saw it on a show. You try to get the thief to strike again. This detective said that thieves never steal just once. They always return to the scene of the crime."

"Here, let's make a list of possible traps we can set," Dani said. "We'll pass it around, and each put one. Okay, number one, baby powder on the floor. That's a classic. The thief walks in it and we can see her footprints." She wrote busily. "More importantly, we can see the residue on their shoes later!"

"And what about a hair across the trunk?" Marisa called out. "We put something else in the trunk, like earrings or something. The thief comes back for *more* goodies. She checks the trunk—and breaks the hair! Then we know someone was here!"

Dani shoved the notebook at her. "That's good, write that down."

Marisa scribbled in the notebook, then passed it to Yael along with the pen. "Your turn," she said.

Yael took the pen and scribbled.

"Okay, read what we've got so far!" Maya called.

Yael froze. She stared down at the book, but she didn't say anything.

"My handwriting's awful," Gracie said. "You probably can't read it at all!"

"Um, I—um. . ." Yael's face grew red. "I can't read any of your stupid handwriting! This game is dumb anyway!" She shoved the notebook off her lap so that it landed on the floor with a flutter of pages. She lurched up from her bunk and out onto the porch. The screen door slammed behind her.

The others stared at each other. "Ah, okay," Dani said. "No problem. Rewind. I'll read it."

But as Dani read, Maya wondered what Yael was thinking out there on the porch. Because she'd been the only one close enough to Yael to see that she was clenching her fists so hard, her knuckles were white— right before she tossed the notebook to the floor.

CHAPTER 8

By dinnertime in the steamy, echoing, noisy chadar
ochel, Yael seemed to have forgotten that she'd been
upset, and Dani didn't mention the notebook again.
Instead, in between bites of drumsticks, noodles, green
beans, and chocolate cookies, they discussed the trap
they'd settled on.

That night, as soon as it was dark, they were all going
to go to the campfire sing together. They'd leave bait—a
pair of Yael's earrings—and make a big deal about how
the cabin would be empty. If the thief was in the area,
she'd probably be waiting for her chance. Tamar rolled
her eyes when they'd told her about the plan but agreed
they could set their traps. If the Eilats—or any other
campers—were going to try again, this might be when
they'd strike. "Listen, guys, we're still going to plow

ahead with our Shabbat practice, you know. Whether we find the stuff or not." She forked some salad. She was wearing a bandanna headband again tonight, and Maya thought how tough it made her look. Very soldierlike.

"Wait, we are?" Yael asked. She shoved her plate away suddenly, even though she'd only taken two bites of her chicken leg.

"Are you done?" Gracie asked with her mouth full. "Can I have your cookie?"

Yael nodded and passed her plate over.

"Of course, we are! Everyone's depending on us." Tamar scraped her plate perfectly clean, then lined up her knife and fork in the middle.

"Don't worry, Tamar," Dani said. "We'll catch the thieves before Friday."

Tamar grinned. "Dani, if you're in charge, I have no doubt you will."

"Well, I'm ready to go to the campfire," Maya said loudly later that night.

"Me too," Dani agreed at the top of her lungs.

"And I'm going to leave these beautiful, expensive earrings right here on my bed," Yael said. "Did I tell you all they're real pearls?" she practically shouted out the window.

Giggling madly, the five Akkos stomped out of the

cabin and into the cricket-chirping night. "Well, I guess the cabin's all empty!" Dani called into the trees. Tamar had already gone ahead to the campfire.

"No one in there?" Marisa asked.

"Nope!" Dani said.

Trying to stifle their laughs, they fled into the nearby trees. Maya could see the cabin path clearly, each with its glowing lights and their own at the end. Groups of girls padded by on the path. "Get off my foot, Gracie!" Maya said.

"Sorry!"

Giggling, Yael crashed over into a shrub. "I can't see anything!"

Dani hauled her up by one arm. "Be serious, you guys! Come on! The thief will never come back to the cabin if they can hear us sneaking around."

Maya crouched down and peered through the screen of branches while the others piled in around her. The path was empty now—everyone was already at the campfire sing. The girls were silent. The wind rustled the leaves around them with a sound like rushing water.

Maya fixed her eyes on the cabin, but she suddenly realized how dark it was on the edge of the woods. The trees stretched way back behind them. Anyone could come out of there. Maya shivered and edged closer to Dani.

Still no sign of the thief—or anyone. Camp seemed

deserted, as if everyone had piled back into busses and gone home. Like they were all alone here, the five of them, with no one around. No one except whoever might be hiding in the woods. Did the Wareloch ever leave Snake Island? Maybe swim across the lake and haul himself, dripping, onto the sand, then creep through the woods—slosh, slosh . . . Waiting to sneak up behind them, slowly, slowly, then lay a cold finger on—

Something big and dark jumped out in front of the cabin, and Maya screamed, falling on Dani. Dani was spooked and lunged forward, smacking into Gracie.

"What is that?!" Yael clutched Marisa.

Marisa screamed. "*Who* is that?"

"A deer! It's only a deer!" Dani yelled, peering through the shrubs again. Yael peeked over Marisa's shoulder. "Just a deer, you guys."

The doe looked up from her grazing, unconcerned, then slowly ambled back into the darkness behind the cabin.

Maya's knees felt weak. Slowly, laughing and exhausted, they disentangled themselves from the bushes and stumbled out onto the path.

"Great trap, Dani," Yael said. She swiped at her hair, which was studded with twigs, and bent down to pick up a bobby pin that had fallen to the ground. "Just one problem—"

"No thief?" Maya broke in.

"No thief," Yael agreed.

"We won't give up!" Dani declared, throwing her fist in the air as they walked toward the warm light of the campfire glowing in the distance. "Holmes always solves his cases—and we will, too."

"Definitely!" Yael agreed. "We're not going to let anyone sabotage Shabbat!"

"Wait, wait!" Gracie grabbed Maya's arm hard and dragged her off the path. "Get down, everyone!"

They crashed back into the bushes. Up ahead, a group of girls was veering off the path toward the campfire and doubling back toward them. The outline of Cori's pith helmet was clearly visible. It was the Eilats.

"OMG, what are they doing?!" Dani scream-whispered right in Maya's ear.

"I don't know!" Maya whispered back. Her heart was hammering.

"They're going back toward the bunks! I can't believe it! Follow them!" Marisa ordered.

"Wait, not on the path, they'll see us!" Yael started fighting her way through some honeysuckle shrubs. "*Argh*—branches, more branches—are there ticks out here?"

"It's like tick central, and be quiet, they're going to hear us!" Gracie shoved Yael aside and took the lead.

The Eilats were coming up to them on the path now,

all laughing quietly to each other. Cori had something in her hand—they all did, Maya realized as the group drew nearer.

"This is it! We were right!" Dani was practically leaping over the bushes in excitement.

"*Shhh!*" Gracie shoved her and they all quieted as the Eilats passed them only a few feet away.

". . . going to freak out when they get back . . ." one of them was saying.

"You got the big ones?" Cori asked.

The Akkos waited, holding their breath, as the Eilats continued down the path. Maya's thighs were trembling from crouching over when Dani signaled that the coast was clear. Stumbling through the brush with the brambles tearing at their legs, they ran through the woods.

The Eilats stopped before the horseshoe of cabins and Maya ducked behind a big bush at the edge of the cabin area. Everyone else piled in behind her. Gradually, Maya peeked out from behind the branches.

The Eilats were shaking something in their hands and then Cori ran over to one of the cabins and sprayed something all over the porch—something puffy and white.

"It's shaving cream!" Yael squealed. "They're doing all the cabins!"

The Eilats were laughing so hard they could hardly stand up while they ran from cabin to cabin, spraying the shaving cream madly all over.

Dani tensed up. "Okay, guys, when they get to ours, we're going to jump out. Are you ready?"

"I'm scared." Marisa hid her face in the back of Maya's shirt.

"Don't be a baby—it's just shaving cream!" Gracie said. The Eilats were getting closer now. "Get ready, you guys. We're about to catch our thieves!"

The cabin porches were dripping with shaving cream now, and Cori was laughing, standing under one of the outside lights, shaking her can, with her pith helmet pushed back on her head. Her face was bright red. "Last one!" she yelled to the group.

She aimed her can at the line of Akko towels on the front porch. As her finger was about to press down, Dani leapt out from behind the shrubs. "HA, GOT YOU!" she yelled.

The other Akkos sprang out too, and Cori spun toward them in a panic. With a wild shriek, she sprayed shaving cream all over Dani's face.

"MY EYES!" Dani screamed. "What are you doing?" The shaving cream was dripping off her nose and chin like she had just been splattered in the face with a cream pie. "What the what!"

"We caught you red-handed, you thieves and

pranksters!" Gracie's hair was sprinkled with twigs and her ponytail was falling out.

"Yeah!" Maya added. "You were going to spray our towels!" This seemed so bold to say but she felt like she could stand up to girls like Cori when she had her fellow Akkos beside her.

"And you stole our Shabbat stuff!" Marisa chimed in. Only Yael was standing quiet, a little behind them all.

Cori lowered her shaving cream can and caught her breath. The rest of the Eilats clustered behind her. "First of all, sorry about your face," she said. She had a raspy voice. "I'm a little crazy, in case you hadn't noticed."

"Yeah, we noticed," Gracie said, her arms folded in front of her. "And you're obnoxious."

Cori nodded agreeably. "True. It's been said. But I'm not a thief. *We're* not thieves." She indicated the Eilats clustered around her.

"Yes, you are! You broke into our cabin and stole the stuff we were going to use to practice for Shabbat!" Dani wiped her face with the bottom of her T-shirt. She still had shaving cream behind her ears.

"What? We didn't do that," a tall girl with hair buzz cut on the sides said. "What are you talking about?"

The other Eilats looked blank. They were honestly confused. After a moment of silence, Maya nudged Dani. "I think they might be telling the truth," she muttered out of the corner of her mouth. Privately, she wondered if she sounded like Watson. There was something about muttering out of the corner of one's mouth that felt very detective-like.

Dani looked around at the other Akkos. Yael was staring hard at the tops of the trees, as if she were looking for a secret agent. But it was dark. The only thing to see was the faint outline of the treetops. Marisa made a "go-ahead" motion with her hands.

Dani stepped forward. She looked hard into Cori's face. Cori blinked, stepped back, and said, "*Whoa.* A little close there, girl-whose-name-I-don't-know."

"*Did. You. Take. Our. Stuff?!*" Dani drilled Cori with her eyes.

"No. We. Did. Not!" Cori said back. She looked right into Dani's face.

"Swear!" the buzz-cut Eilat said. "We just wanted to prank everyone, like for an opening-camp thing. That's all!"

Dani sighed. Maya did too. "All right. Fine. I believe you."

"Me too," Marisa chimed in, and the others nodded.

"Great! Thanks for the vote of confidence!" Cori shook her can of shaving cream and aimed it at the Akkos. Yael shrieked and retreated, and Cori howled her raspy laugh.

"Misfire, guys," Dani said as they walked slowly back down the path. The campfire was still going on. Maya could see the glow of the flames and hear the guitar up ahead.

"It wasn't them," Maya said. She should have felt let down but, oddly, she didn't. She linked her arm with Dani's. It must be that she was with her group. *Her group.* That was a nice thought. She'd never really had a group before, and now, here she was. It felt like nothing could be too scary or boring with the Akkos around her. She thought back to the winter night in her room and the paper Mom had thrust at her. She had no idea then, how quickly Shalom would feel like home.

The counselors were playing cards in the pavilion. Tamar was out there too. Lying in her bunk late that night, Maya could hear them through the screen, laughing and talking. She tried to figure out what game they were playing. Euchre, maybe? Poker? There was clinking, so maybe they were playing for quarters?

All around her the cabin was filled with the sounds of breathing. Gracie was making a little noise like a whistling kettle. Yael mumbled something that sounded like "candy blast." Outside, the insects were sawing and singing and chirping. Why did anyone ever say the woods were quiet at night? It was way noisier out here than at home.

Then Maya heard a new noise—a kind of snuffling. She lifted her head off the pillow. It was snuffling and some kind of breathing but not the sleeping kind. It was coming from the top bunk.

Carefully, Maya edged out from under her sleeping bag. She eased herself up the ladder until she could see Dani, sitting up in her bed, with her arms wrapped around her drawn-up knees.

"Hey," Maya whispered. She crawled across the bed, trying not to rustle too much.

Dani looked up. In the gleam of the moonlight from the window Maya could see tears spilling down her cheeks. Maya held her finger to her lips, then as softly as she could, dropped over the side of her bunk onto the floor. She motioned to Dani, who slid out from under her sleeping bag. She stepped on her shower shoes and stumbled. Yael snorted in her sleep, and both of them froze. Then Yael's breathing smoothed out, and Maya exhaled. She and Dani crept out of the cabin, easing the screen door open and closing it with exquisite care.

Outside was big and cool and filled with the noise of the forest. The moon sailed overhead like some gorgeous glowing ship. Dani sank down under a pine tree in the middle of the horseshoe, and Maya sat beside her. "What's wrong?" Maya asked.

Dani gulped. "Nothing. I'm fine." She had her mom's picture in her hand.

"No, you're not. You were crying in your bed."

Dani didn't say anything. She buried her face in her drawn-up knees.

Maya put a tentative hand on her back. "Come on. Are you homesick?"

Dani gulped. "A little. I knew this would happen. I just miss my mom so much." Her voice trailed off into a whisper. "And my own bed."

"It's the worst feeling." Maya said. "It's like—"

"A stomach pit with no bottom," Dani broke in.

"Yes! Like a hole carved out of the middle of you. Why do you always feel it in your stomach? That's what I want to know." Maya eased the picture out of her friend's hand and studied it. "Your mom looks really nice."

"She is. She's *um*—" Dani gulped. "She gives good hugs."

"Listen!" Maya broke in, before Dani could start crying again. "I have a great way to feel better. I mean, it won't cure you, but maybe you'll just be able to go to sleep tonight."

"What?"

"You close your eyes."

Dani looked at her.

"Close them!"

Dani shut her eyes.

"Okay, now pretend I'm your mom."

Dani opened her eyes. "*Whaaa*?"

"Trust me! This is a great idea. Instead of me, just picture your mom, sitting right here on the ground with us."

Dani rolled her eyes but closed them. "This is a little weird."

"Now, I'm going to give you a hug, but you have to pretend it's your mom, not me. That's the key."

"Fine!" Dani whispered. "But this is *not* going to work."

"Maybe not, but at least it's better than crying." Maya leaned forward and wrapped her arms around her friend. She thought about her own mother and gave Dani the kind of hug her mom would give.

Dani opened her eyes.

"Did it work?"

"*Umm* . . . well, you're kind of bony. My mom's more squishy. And you smell different. Not bad! Just different." Dani grinned. "But I do feel better."

"See? Success!" Maya raised her hand for a silent high five. "Are you going to be able to go to sleep now?"

Dani nodded. "I think so. Thanks."

They crept back into the cabin. Everyone was still asleep. Dani climbed back up into her bunk and Maya wiggled under her sleeping bag. She listened until she could hear the sounds of regular breathing from above her. Then she pushed her face into her pillow comfortably and let sleep wash over her.

CHAPTER 9

Two days of tie-dye, kickball, decorate-your-counselor, and climbing wall, and the Shabbat items were still missing. They were no closer to catching the thief. They'd tried everything. Gracie suggested sprinkling baby powder on the floor when everyone was at dinner. But when they came back to check, they only found the tiny footprints of a mouse that had apparently been making his home in the bottom of Marisa's mattress. Then they found out that the reason the mouse was making his home in Marisa's mattress was that she had a whole pack of Twizzlers hidden under there. The mouse had delicately nibbled through the bag and enjoyed most of a Twizzler before they found him. He'd also pooped all over the floor under the bed, and Yael had to be talked down from Dani's top bunk, where she'd gone to hide.

Then they had deployed the hair trick Marisa had

suggested, just to see if anyone was going through their things. Dani had carefully taped Yael's hair, because it was the longest, across the latch of the trunk. When they'd checked on it after lunch, the hair was broken. Everyone had screamed and clutched each other until Tamar, coming in after them, had pointed out that she had opened the trunk an hour earlier, looking for the spare sheets. "Holmes would never let this happen," Dani had said, sighing. And everyone else seemed to agree.

Then at lunch, Gracie came over waving a piece of paper. "Guys, guys, guys, it's here!" She slapped the paper down on the lunch table. Maya leaned over her turkey sandwich to see.

"*Camp Shalom News*," the banner headline read.

"*Oooohhh!*" Maya breathed. "Is it in there? Our ad?"

Everyone else was craning to look too. Marisa was leaning on Maya's back, practically pressing her into her own plate.

"There it is!" Dani pointed to the page halfway down. "She put it in."

"Of course, she did," Rachel said, suddenly appearing behind them as if she'd been conjured. "What do you think, that I wouldn't do it? Unless there's some reason you didn't want the ad used, *Dani*."

Maya twisted around and looked Rachel full in the

face. What? Why was she saying Dani's name like that?

Rachel met Maya's eyes in a challenging way. What was with her? She was so unpleasant. Rachel gave her a little smile, as if she knew exactly what Maya was thinking, and headed back to the Haifa table, where Annie and the others were eating their own turkey sandwiches.

"Okay, guys, this is important," Dani was saying. "Everyone's reading the paper. *Watch their faces.* Does anyone look suspicious? Does anyone look guilty? This is our chance to pick up more clues." Dani's face was intense.

Everyone nodded and started scanning the dining hall. Every camper had a copy of the newspaper on the table in front of them. Maya tried to study each face, but everyone was just eating. One of the Eilats got up to refill the chip bowl. That wasn't suspicious, even though she was taking a lot of chips. Some people were reading the paper beside their plates. Some were ignoring it. Someone at the little girls' table spilled a whole glass of cranberry juice, and there were shrieks and the shuffle of paper towels.

"Ha! What about her?" Marisa stage whispered. She hid her hand half under the table and pointed at a girl who was heading purposefully for the door, with the newspaper in hand.

"That's Annie!" Maya said. "She's so nice. She'd never steal anything."

"We can't be too sure," Dani said, low. "Marisa, you want to follow her?"

Marisa got up and started making her way through the maze of tables. Suddenly, she ducked down, hunching over and scurrying like a crab.

Maya groaned. "What is she doing? She'll give us away!"

Dani sighed. "At least no one's noticing."

"You're joking, right?" Gracie said. Marisa was still duckwalking behind Annie. Everyone in the dining hall was watching and laughing.

Maya sighed. "Maybe she's not the best secret agent there ever was?" She watched Marisa duckwalk out the door after Annie.

The Akkos waited. Gracie giggled nervously and then was quiet. "How do you know that girl?" Yael asked.

"She was on our bus. Do you remember her?" Maya said.

Yael shook her head and picked at her fingers, then raised one to her mouth and nibbled at the nail. Maya noticed all her other fingernails were bitten down too. One was down to the quick. She winced and looked away. Someone should tell Yael to stop biting like that. It looked like it really hurt.

Marisa barged back into the dining hall and ran over

to them. She collapsed on the bench beside Gracie, out of breath.

"Well?" Dani demanded.

Marisa shook her head, catching her breath. "She went to the bathroom."

Everyone groaned.

Tamar got up and started clattering plates around. "Come on, ladies, enough sleuthing for right now. It's time for ropes course!"

"I'm not sure this is such a good idea!" Maya called out. She was clinging to a rope net, with another rope beneath her feet. A bright red helmet was clamped to her head. The only thing between her and the treetops twenty feet below was the harness around her shoulders, waist, and legs. It felt uncomfortably like a tight diaper. But she felt a little safer since she was clipped into a rope line with a carabiner the size of her fist.

"Is this supposed to be fun?" Dani stared at the ground from a little platform several feet away. Sweat glistened on her forehead as she clutched the platform pole. "People think this is fun?"

It was the Akko's first time on the high ropes course, and Tamar had demonstrated how they could climb through the web of prickly ropes to reach the end, where there was a zip line that ran to a wide platform over the roofs of the cabins. The zip line *did* look fun, Maya had to admit, and even now, she could hear Gracie's joyous scream as she sailed down the line.

"Okay, Maya, come on across the net," Tamar coaxed now, leaning back against her own harness. Maya gritted her teeth and forced herself to let go of the prickly rope with one hand and shuffle one more foot toward Tamar. The trees yawned beneath her.

"*Whooaaa. . .*" She teetered on the rope.

"The harness will hold you!" Tamar called. "I promise!"

"But maybe it won't?" Maya called back. "Are we one hundred percent sure?"

"One hundred percent," Tamar reassured her. She stretched out a strong tanned hand. "Come on. I'm right here."

"Girl, go!" Dani shouted behind her. "I can't move until you do, and I'm not staying up here one minute longer than I have to."

"*Yaaaayyyyy!*" Through the trees, Maya could see Yael zipping joyfully down the line. Once you got there, you had the ropes counselor to help you unhook. That moment couldn't come soon enough, as far as Maya was concerned.

She grabbed Tamar's hand and shuffled left until she reached the next platform. Dani edged up behind her a moment later.

"I'm a city girl, you know," Dani muttered as she

sank down gratefully on the solid wood surface. "I'm supposed to be skateboarding. Or maybe going to a Broadway show."

"You're from Cincinnati," Maya pointed out. "There's no Broadway. And you don't know how to skateboard."

"Yeah, but think about what a good time this would be to start." Dani picked a rope fiber out of her hair.

"Come on, girls!" Tamar shouted. "Your turn on the zip line."

Olive, the ropes counselor, clipped a line onto the front of Maya's harness. "The harness will hold you, no matter what," she assured Maya.

"Even if I just fall off the platform?"

"Even if you literally jump straight off the platform. You're clipped in. See?"

Olive stepped right off the platform into thin air, and before Maya could scream like any sensible person would, her ropes counselor was dangling and smiling a foot below the platform, leaning back in her harness with her legs outstretched. "See?" She stretched her arms wide. "You're totally safe."

"*Whoa*, okay." Maya gripped the line on the front of her harness.

"Now you try," Olive said.

"Wait, what?"

"Try hopping off the platform. It'll give you confidence."

Olive was clearly crazy. Maya was not going to hop off the platform.

"Come on!" Olive motioned from her dangling perch. "It's fun! And you'll feel better after."

Maya clutched the rope hard with her sweaty hands. *Ohhh.* The ground was *so* far away. She looked down and stepped off. There was one terrifying second of falling, and amazingly, in that moment she had time to thoroughly regret her decision—and then the harness caught her rear and her legs, snapping up around them and holding her up in midair—just like Olive said.

"*Whooaaa*, I'm doing it!" she yelled, twisting on her rope.

"Maya, no! Death is not the answer!" Dani yelled from above her.

Maya looked up. Her friend had arrived on the platform and was gazing down at her.

"Olive was giving me more confidence in my ropes," she explained.

"Now, just reach for the platform and climb back on." Olive demonstrated.

"I think we've been at camp too long," Dani murmured. "This stuff is getting a little crazy."

Maya gazed down at the campsite below. From up there she could see a maze of brown dirt paths leading in and around each cabin. At one end, she could see the path leading to the lake, then the lake itself, looking like a flat metal plate on this windless, overcast morning. Then she squinted and could see the meadow in the far distance. On the other side of the meadow, the path led to the office and the big green lawn at the entrance. With her eyes she followed the gravel path around again from the office, through the grove of trees to the chadar ochel, then to the shower house, and back to the cabins. It was cool. "Look, there's Akko," she said to Dani, pointing to their cabin, with its swim towels draped on the porch railing. She could even see her own, the red starburst one on the end.

"I'm ready to be down there on my own bunk," Dani said from behind her.

"You guys are doing great," Olive said. "Ready for the zip line? You hang on here, okay?" Olive showed Maya a red rubber handgrip on the line. "Just lift your feet up and go!"

Maya squeezed her eyes shut and leaned forward. For a fraction of a second she was sure the harness had broken and she was falling, and then the nylon straps pressed into her flesh, holding her up. She was soaring through the tallest trees in a dizzying kaleidoscope of green. "*Whhooaaa!*" she shrieked, clinging to the handgrip. "I'm gonnaaaaa diiiiie!" Below her, the cabin roofs whizzed by. Then she caught the briefest glimpse of something else—someone with dark hair, going up the steps of Akko. She only had time to think, *What?*, before she thumped onto the big, solid, wide-cushioned platform at the end.

"*Yaaaeeeee!*" Dani crashed into her from behind.

"One at a time, ladies!" Olive yelled from the head of the zip line.

"Dani!" Maya got to her knees. "I saw—I saw—" She paused to catch her breath. "Someone going into the cabin!" No one was supposed to be in the cabins during activity periods—it was a camp rule.

"Hurry!" Dani struggled to unclip her harness. "They might be returning to the scene of the crime! We have to go investigate! Quick! Before they leave!" She managed to release her line clip, and both girls shed their harnesses and skittered down the wooden steps to the cabins.

Panting, they ran along the dirt foot path to Akko. "Maybe they're putting the Shabbat stuff back!" Maya panted.

"Either way, we'll find out who it is!" Dani called back over her shoulder.

The screen door of the cabin was open. Dani threw her arm across Maya's stomach as they mounted the steps. "*Shhh!* We don't want to scare them off!"

Maya nodded. They crept forward. The sound of rustling came from inside.

"Got you!" Dani shouted, leaping forward and pushed the screen open.

Max turned around. He was holding a clipboard.

"Hi, girls! How was ropes?"

Dani's shoulder sagged. "It's just you."

"Yep!" Max answered. "Just doing cabin inspection. Kind of messy in here. So, guess what?—You guys get the dirty sock award!" He held up the dark gray gym sock. "See you girls at lunch—and have fun doing kitchen patrol!"

The screen door banged shut behind him, and Dani sank onto a bunk. "I really thought we were going to catch the thief."

Maya put her arm around her friend's shoulders. "Well, we apprehended Max. Doesn't that count for something?"

"And we got the dirty sock award!" Dani groaned. She poked at the sock lying on Tamar's bunk. "This thing looks like it's been run over by a garbage truck."

Maya grimaced. "Does it smell or is that just me?"

"It smells like failure." Dani flopped back on Yael's bed dramatically, arms outstretched. Something crackled under her arm. "Hey, what's this?" From under the edge of the blanket, Dani pulled out a little memo pad, like the kind Maya's mom would write the grocery list on. She flipped the cover open and scanned the pages.

"Dani, stop, that's Yael's!" Maya said.

"I know, sorry." Dani clapped the cover closed. "That was dumb—I don't know what I was thinking."

"You saw something though," Maya said. "I can tell by your face."

"Yeah . . ." Dani looked troubled now. "Something."

"Okay, you have to tell me."

But before Dani could say anything, the screen door banged open and everyone else poured in, clattering and talking. Just in time, Dani quickly shoved Yael's notebook back under her blanket.

Marisa shrieked when she saw the dirty sock, and then everyone had to inspect it before Tamar informed them that it was time for lunch . . . and for their collective humiliation. Before Maya knew it, she was being carried along on a tide of talk and laughter and indignation right to the door of the dining hall.

CHAPTER 10

After everyone had served themselves grilled cheese and apples, Max reminded them that ping-pong games had to stop *when dinner announcements were made* and not fifteen minutes after. Then Damien led them in "I Had Three Little Goats," and after that, Max took the mic again.

"Now, it's time for . . . the dirty sock award!" he announced. "Our most adorable but also messiest cabin for the day is . . . Akko!"

Everyone cheered and banged the tables. Marisa took the dirty sock out of the plastic bag they'd stuffed it in, and marched forward, holding her nose theatrically. Everyone laughed and she placed it upside down on the wooden dowel on the stand beside Max. "Enjoy lunch cleanup!" Max said, grinning at them. "Grilled cheese day is the best!"

The Akkos groaned while the rest of the campers clapped.

"You know, dishes aren't really my thing," Yael remarked half an hour later in the steamy kitchen. The staff had shown them what to do with all the plates and glasses and forks, and then had left. "Really, my thing is going to the pool."

"Well, right now, your thing is scraping all these plates and stacking them here," Tamar said, clearing off a section of counter. "Then Gracie and I will load the dishwasher and, Marisa, you load the silverware. Dani and Maya, you guys get out there and wipe the tables." She handed them each a small bucket with bleach-smelling hot water with a rag floating in it.

The tables were scattered with toast crumbs and bits of cheese and sticky places where the apple slices had landed. Maya dipped her rag in her bucket and wrung it out. "Okay, we're alone," she said to Dani, who was looking at the table with disgust. "Tell me."

"This is just nasty," Dani said, starting to wipe. "People are pigs." She looked at Maya. "Wait, tell you what?"

"You know what." Maya looked around. Everyone was still in the kitchen. "What you saw in Yael's notebook."

"Oh, that." Dani kept wiping, her eyes on the table. "Yeah."

"Come on." It was wrong, Maya knew that. Wrong and nosy. But she couldn't help it. Or maybe she didn't want to help it. Either way, it was the same feeling that she had when she skipped to the end of a really, really good book. She just *had to know*.

"Fine." Dani swiped at the table. "It said, *I can't. I just can't do it. No, no, no.*" She dipped her rag in her bucket and wrung it out. "Her writing is pretty big and round, so it was easy to read."

"*I can't?*" Maya thought. "What does that mean? Can't what?"

Dani moved down the table. She'd wiped around the crumbs pretty successfully. They were all still on the table. "I don't know."

I can't. Maya pondered as she scrubbed. What could someone like Yael not do? She seemed like the type who could do anything. But apparently not. There was something she couldn't do, and Maya had no idea what.

"So, we're not still leading Shabbat, right?" Yael asked after kitchen patrol as over. She fidgeted with her hair, taking out one of the long bobby pins and sticking it back in again. They were all sitting on the floor of the amphitheater by the lake, still sweaty from a game of charades. In front of them, empty wooden benches stretched up the hill. Behind them, the lake shimmered. This was where the camp welcomed the start of Shabbat every week. Tamar had already told them how special it was when everyone was dressed in their one nice outfit, the leaders were at the front with their guitars, and everyone sang the blessings.

Maya thought Yael sounded kind of hopeful. Maybe she thought the Shabbat stuff was too much like school. The thought had occurred to Maya, too, a couple of times.

Tamar smiled. "We definitely are. We'll just forge ahead."

"What?" Yael looked shocked. "That's crazy! We-we won't be able to practice!"

"Yeah, that's not fair," Marisa chimed in.

"Fair or not, we'll just make the best of it," Tamar said, sounding very authoritative. "We have to be tough, right, girls?"

Everyone reluctantly nodded.

"We'll just pretend for now," Maya said.

"Good idea, Maya." Tamar took a sheaf of papers out of her backpack. "Now, we all know the Shabbat blessings by heart, right? But at Camp Shalom, we like to add our own poems to read. It's a really beautiful way to welcome Shabbat." She unfolded the papers and smoothed them out. "Everyone will get a poem, and we can each practice reading aloud, okay? This will be your poem at the ceremony and we'll each get a turn to read. You first, Maya." Tamar handed her a paper.

"*Tonight on Shabbat, we gather as one,*" Maya read aloud.

"Louder," Tamar advised. "We've got to be really loud."

Maya nodded. "*The Sabbath bride is welcome. Beauty and peace fill our souls.*" She tried to imagine the empty benches in front of them filled with campers and her voice soaring above all of them.

"Great!" Tamar said. "Okay, your turn, Yael." She offered Yael a poem.

Yael took the paper slowly, as if it might explode. She peered down at the page.

"Go ahead," Tamar encouraged. "*This sacred time . . .*"

"These words are really little," Yael said. "It's hard to see them." Maya saw her swallow. "*Um . . .*"

The pause stretched out. In the distance, Maya could see girls in the kayaks like little colored dots on the expanse of blue lake.

"*Um . . .*" Yael said again.

Dani looked at Maya. *What's wrong with her?* she mouthed. Maya shook her head.

Then the clanging bell that signaled the end of the

activity period sounded. Yael shoved the paper toward Tamar "There's the bell! Don't we have archery now?"

Tamar looked at her arm where she always wrote their schedule in permanent marker. "Swimming."

Maya's stomach fell into her shoes with a thunk.

CHAPTER 11

The lake was all sparking blue, brightly painted kayaks, shouting girls jumping off the raft, and occasionally, a massive splash as someone soared down the homemade slide that ran all the way through the woods.

"Kayaks, Akkos!" Leah, the swimming counselor called. "Two per boat! We're going go once around the lake—that's about halfway to Snake Island."

"The overnight!" Marisa shuddered. "I really don't like sleeping on the ground."

"I don't mind it," Yael said, and everyone looked at her in surprise.

"*Um*, I thought you had allergies and got migraines!" Dani said, somewhat accusingly.

Yael shrugged. "I'm not allergic to outside. My dad used to take us camping every weekend when we lived in Cambridge. We'd go up to the Cape and camp on the beach." She looked around at everyone staring. "What?"

"Pair up!" the swim counselor called. "Everyone grab a kayak from the rack next to the oar house."

"Hang on," Tamar said. "Sorry, Maya, not you."

Maya swallowed. Not a shock exactly, but it still felt like she'd been scolded like a disobedient puppy.

"We'll do a swim lesson, okay?" Tamar was trying to be nice, but it just made Maya feel worse. Tamar put her hands on Maya's shoulders. "You just have to practice a little more. We can't let you go on the Snake Island sleepover unless you're safe in the water."

"*Um*, I do know how to swim," Maya choked out, not looking at Tamar. She tried to stuff down the fear rising up in her.

"I know you do." Tamar's voice was gentle. "But we've got to work on getting you to relax in the water. That'll help with your basic skills." Tamar eyed Maya.

Maya kept her eyes fixed on the beach. Weird that this was the only place in camp with sand. *Keep thinking those thoughts! Then you won't cry!* She couldn't cry in front of a former Israeli army soldier. And she definitely couldn't tell her she was scared of the *water*. Like a stupid baby.

"Here, how about using this?" Leah said. She held out a kickboard.

Maya took it, feeling like she was about five. She didn't look at anyone else. Of course, they were staring, but at least she didn't have to see it.

"Okay, now, stretch the board out in front of you, like this." Leah demonstrated. Did she have to talk so loud? Was she a sports announcer in another life? The others were already paddling around the lake in the brightly colored kayaks.

Miserably, Maya held her arms out in front of her. She swallowed hard. The fear was twisting inside her again.

"Now, keep your arms out and support your upper body with the board," Leah went on.

"I know how to swim," Maya mumbled to the board.

Leah didn't hear her. "Lift your feet off the bottom and kick!" she bellowed, just in case there was anyone who hadn't heard by now. "Come on! The raft's not going to come to you!"

With her breath coming faster now, Maya gripped the slimy fabric covering the board. She leaned on it gingerly, feeling the chilly brown lake water lapping up around her arms. The mud sucked at her feet.

"Now kick!" Leah shouted.

Maya lifted one foot off the lake bottom. Then her hands slipped, and the kickboard popped straight up into the air. Her feet went up and her head went down, under the water, into the darkness. Gasping, she flailed, searching for the top, sucking in water, when she felt a strong hand under her arm.

Leah hauled her up as she staggered to her feet. "Okay? What happened?"

Maya coughed. "I slipped," she choked out, raking her wet hair back from her face. "I'm—I'm okay." Her heart was hammering in her ears.

Leah studied her for a long moment, then nodded. "Okay. Why don't you take five?"

Maya nodded and staggered out of the lake. She sank down on the sun-warmed strip of beach and stared at the merry kayakers calling out, flicking water onto each other from their paddles. Dani and Gracie were trying to knock their kayak into Marisa's. Maya sighed and put her head down on her updrawn knees. She felt heavy and flat and stupid.

A shadow covered the sun, and Maya looked up. Yael was standing there. Before Maya could say anything, she plopped down beside her.

"How come you're not in a kayak?" Maya asked. She wished Yael would go away. She didn't feel like talking.

"I don't know. I was going to, then I saw you sitting here."

"You mean you saw me looking stupid in the water." It came out harsher than she intended.

Yael shrugged again. "You want me to do your hair?"

She pulled a comb out of the pocket of the gym shorts she wore over her suit.

"Um . . ." But Yael had already knelt up behind her and was enthusiastically pulling the comb through Maya's wet, lake-smelling hair.

"Here, you know what would look really cute?" Yael said. "This kind of French twist my cousin showed me. You can do it on short hair too."

"Ah!" Maya sputtered as the comb hit a knot. Her head was being tugged back.

"Sorry!" Yael took one of her long bobby pins out of her own hair and did something twisty to Maya's. She pushed the bobby pin in so that it slid against Maya's scalp. "There!" She dug a little pocket mirror out of her pocket and held it up in front of Maya's face. "What do you think?"

Maya took the mirror and turned her head to the side. Her normally fuzzy, wavy hair was smooth and slicked back with a sleek knot at the nape of her neck. "It looks . . . good!" she said. "Fancy." It did look pretty. Prettier than she'd ever seen her own hair actually. She grinned. "Wow, thanks." She handed the mirror back to Yael. The kayakers were back. They were dragging the boats up onto the sand.

"Yeah! We can do another style later," Yael said, jumping to her feet and hoisting Maya up by the hand.

"I love doing hair. Actually, I was thinking of being a stylist one day and owning my own salon and—"

Suddenly a shriek split the air. It was Dani, standing beside the oar house, the door open beside her, her hands plastered over her mouth. "Tamar! Come quick! Hurry!"

Maya and Yael looked at each other with wide eyes. "Come on!" Maya said and started running across the sand.

CHAPTER 12

"What?"

"Dani, what is it?" The Akkos ran up from the beach.

"The—the practice cup and the candlesticks!" Dani held them out. The challah cover and the candles were there too. "I was putting my oars away, and I knocked over a bunch in the corner, and there they were, just sitting there!"

Tamar took them and shook out the challah cover. "This is them all right. But what are they doing in the oar house?"

The girls were quiet. Maya rubbed one sandy foot against another. Yael giggled suddenly and then was silent. Finally, Dani spoke up. "Well, the thief must have hidden them there."

The thief! Everyone glanced at each other.

"I wish I could think of another explanation." Tamar fixed each Akko with a piercing eye. "And why were you in the oar house, Dani?"

What! Did she suspect *Dani*?

Dani must have thought the same thing because a blotchy red flushed her cheeks. "I had an old oar, so Leah told me to put it in here instead of with the others."

"I did," Leah chimed in from behind them. "I'm trying to keep the old ones and the new ones separate."

Tamar nodded. "Well, we have the items back now. That's what's important. Now we can practice properly."

"Good!" Gracie said.

"Yeah, great!" Yael echoed. Her smile was huge and toothy. "Awesome! I was really worried there."

Dani gave Yael a quick look Maya couldn't read. What was she thinking?

Maya nudged Dani as they headed up the path. "What?" she whispered.

Dani shook her head. "Nothing. Never mind."

Later, at dinner, they went over what they knew.

"We know there's a thief now," Dani said between bites of her burger with pickles. "Holmes would tell us we have two questions now: *who* is our thief? And *what* is her motive?"

"It's obviously not one of us," Gracie said. "That would be just too weird."

"That makes the most sense," Dani agreed. "Someone else would have to be going in and out of the cabin."

"And anyone can sneak in," Yael put in. She sat at the end of the table, a little apart from the others. "It's not like the cabins are locked."

"That's true," Maya said. "I don't think we should rule anyone out." She narrowed her eyes and looked around the noisy, crowded dining hall. Someone started a cheer at the other end of the room and everyone else began banging their spoons. She raised her voice over the noise. "Anyone could be a suspect."

Just then, Elise, the song leader, climbed onto a chair at the other end of the room and started "If I Had a Hammer" with her guitar. Everyone cheered. All the Akkos leapt to their feet. "Okay, this side, you're line one," Elise yelled over the noise. "And this side, you're line two. Go!"

She started strumming, amplified by the microphone. "If I had a hammer—"

"I'd hammer in the morning," Maya sang, her arm draped around Dani's neck on one side, and Gracie's on the other. She sang as loud as she could. It seemed like camp was the only place you could sing as loud as you wanted. Her voice vibrated in her chest and blended with the big stew of sound echoing in the dining hall. She wasn't thinking of swimming or of the thief or of anything except how good it felt to sing with her friends.

Something was outside. Maya swam up out of layers of sleep and through the gauze she heard low murmurs, rustling, and sniffing sounds. Something was outside. She held very still, gripping the edge of her sleeping bag with both hands, and straining her ears. Someone was outside the window, maybe two someones. The night breeze blew across her face and then the frogs started up. They were making it hard to hear.

"Maya!"

Gracie was sitting up on her lower bunk, her hair falling on her shoulders. "Something's outside!" she whispered.

"I heard it," Maya whispered back.

"Do you think it's an animal?" Gracie clicked on her flashlight and shined it around the cabin. The white beam flashed on the walls, the floor, then Yael's bed, where she was visible as a long unmoving lump under her sleeping bag, then Tamar's bed. It was empty.

"Maybe it's Tamar outside," Maya whispered. "I'll go check." She slid out from under her sleeping bag, trying not to rustle too much. Easing the screen door open, she strained her eyes into the blackness beyond the porch. The moon was up, and in a moment, her eyes adjusted.

She let the screen door close softly and padded to the end of the porch.

Two figures were standing in the horseshoe area in front of the cabins—one tall and one short. They were talking, and the short one was sniffling. Maya could hear her clearly. Then they came toward the cabin. It was Dani and Tamar. Maya didn't have time to move before they saw her.

"What are you doing up?" Tamar scolded, sweeping past her into the cabin. "Go to bed."

Dani's face was streaked with tears just visible in the moonlight.

"What's going on?" Maya whispered. "What happened?"

Dani shook her head. "I can't tell you now. But Maya, I'm in huge trouble."

CHAPTER 13

"So what happened last night?" Maya asked Dani in the morning. They were playing gaga, and the pit was hot and dusty. "I couldn't fall asleep for forever after you and Tamar came back. I was so worried!"

They were crowded around the wooden enclosure, watching the other Akkos slap the ball back and forth with the Haifas. The idea was to hit the ball with one hand, but not let it hit you below the waist. If it did, you were out. It was an Israeli game and pretty fun—also noisy. Right now, girls were pressed all around them, yelling. Maya figured the noise was enough cover.

"Maya, it was awful," Dani said. Her eyes were puffy, and she kept them fixed on the gaga pit. "I snuck out."

"What!" Maya gasped "Why?" Dani just wasn't the sneaking-out type.

"I was lying there, holding my picture, and I couldn't stand it. I missed home so badly. I thought if I snuck over to the office, I could call my mom really quickly. I just wanted to hear her voice."

Maya inhaled. "So did you do it?"

In the pit, Rachel smacked the ball out, and the Akkos cheered. Rachel scowled, her sweaty curls clinging to her forehead. Her glasses were all fogged up and coated with dust. Maya wondered how she could see anything.

"There's that phone in the hallway. I saw it that first day. It's on the wall by that tree sculpture. I didn't think anyone would hear me if I whispered."

"Max said that was only for emergencies!"

"Maya! You're in!" Tamar called.

"Hang on for one second," Maya told Dani. She climbed over the wooden enclosure and positioned herself by the wall.

"GA–GA!" everyone yelled, and Annie served the ball. Maya leaped forward and swatted it toward Yael, who batted it at Marisa's feet. Marisa danced away, hitting the ball hard toward Maya. She jumped, but it hit her shins anyway.

"You're out, Maya," Tamar ruled.

Maya climbed back over the enclosure, and Dani fixed her with a knowing eye. "Did you let it hit you on purpose?"

"No comment." Maya grabbed Dani's elbow and edged her back into the crowd of girls a little more. She leaned her head next to her friend's. "So, what happened?"

"What happened is, I forgot all about the counselor room."

"It's down the hall!" The counselor room was a big, wood-paneled screened porch with a bunch of falling-apart easy chairs and couches, a bookcase stuffed with moldy magazines, and a TV that looked like it was from 1800. The counselors went there to relax after lights out. Yael claimed they were playing poker for money, but Maya thought they probably just ate candy and drank soda.

"I know. So, I got over there and I'm dialing the phone and I'm so nervous. And then my mom answered, and I just totally fell apart when I heard her voice, and I was bawling, so I didn't even hear Tamar coming out of the counselor room. My mom calmed me down and then I hung up and turned around, and Tamar was standing right there."

"What did she say?" Maya gasped.

"She was like, 'What are you doing out of bed? You're in big trouble.' And I was like, 'I was calling my mom.'"

"Then what happened?"

"I don't know, she just told me to get back and get to bed, and we'd talk in the morning." Dani looked desperate. "What do you think they'll do? Send me home?"

"No, they can't!"

Annie scored the last point, with a win for the Haifas. Then gaga was over, and everyone was filtering out for lunch. They were almost to the door of the dining hall. Maya pulled it open, and they were swallowed up in a sea of laughing, chattering campers all streaming in. "They won't send you home. Maybe they'll just call your parents." Then she realized what she'd just said and cracked up.

"Very funny. Maybe they'll—" Dani stopped short. In front of them a crowd of campers were standing still too. Max, Tamar, and two other counselors were standing up on chairs. They were talking quietly to each other. And with one look at their faces, Maya could tell something was very wrong. She'd never seen Max look so serious.

"What? What's happening?" Maya whispered to Gracie, coming up next to her.

"I don't know! They just told everyone to listen up!"

"Quiet!" Max called. "We have a serious problem to discuss!"

The campers hushed.

"Sometime between yesterday at lunch time and today, someone—we don't know who—took the keys from my office. They unlocked the storage closet and took the lockbox that holds the camp's silver Shabbat candlesticks and kiddush cup. As you know, these are extremely meaningful and valuable camp items."

Everyone turned to look at them. Maya blushed. Yael's face was scarlet also. She was staring straight ahead at Max, not looking at anyone. Beside Maya, Dani was standing perfectly still also, her mouth set in a grimace.

"I hope that no one would do this as a prank. If for some terribly misguided reason, stealing these items is your idea of fun, you must return them immediately. But I know Shalom campers pretty well. And the campers I know would never take a joke too far." Max put his papers down on the table in front of him. "That leaves me only with the conclusion that this terrible act is a theft. I don't know why. I don't know how. But I do know that this is very, very serious. Perhaps the most serious thing that has ever happened at camp. We are considering this a robbery," he went on. "And unfortunately, the police will have to be involved, *unless* we can find the items. If you know anything at all, if you hear anything at all, please come talk to us. We'll keep your confidence. That will be all. Your counselors will have further instructions." He stepped down from the chair.

The campers erupted, murmuring and talking as everyone started filtering through the food line and finding their tables. Maya and Dani grabbed tuna sandwiches and joined the rest of the Akkos.

"Tamar, what's going to happen?" Marisa asked, tearing her sandwich into little pieces with her fingers. She started dipping them into a blob of mustard one by one.

"We're going to have to find the stolen items," Tamar said, her face serious. "And just as important—who took them."

"Do you think Max will really call the police?" Gracie asked.

Tamar fixed them all with a stare. "This is very serious. Our cabin has already had one theft. We didn't know if it was a prank or not, and we still don't know. We only found the items by chance. Now something really valuable and special is gone. What's more, this time, the thief stole the keys from Max's office and unlocked the lockbox!" She set her cup down with a thunk. "I don't know if someone is out to get the Akkos, or what. All I know is that there've been two thefts since camp started, and both have to do with us as Shabbat leaders."

At the end of the table, there was a sudden clatter. Yael had knocked over her glass of lemonade. "Sorry! Sorry," she mumbled, scrambling for napkins.

Tamar stood up. "Dani, come with me please."

The Akkos all grew quiet. Maya watched her friend's face go pale. "Okay," Dani said hesitantly. She followed Tamar into the hall. The bottom fell out of Maya's stomach. There was one reason she could think of why Tamar might want to talk to Dani in private.

"What's going on?" Marisa whispered. Her eyes were round. "Is she in trouble?" Maya could see it—Marisa realized what Dani could be in trouble for the minute the words left her mouth. Maya saw the recognition roll across Marisa's face. The others did too. Yael looked up, her mouth open. Then she closed it with a snap and looked away.

"No! She's not in trouble!" Maya bit into her sandwich. "And be quiet about it. You don't know anything, even if you think you do."

"Sorry." Marisa's eyes grew suspiciously shiny and she looked away.

Regret washed over Maya. "No, I'm sorry." She never should have opened her mouth.

As they were leaving the dining hall, Maya found Dani standing near the door. She grabbed her friend and propelled her over to the side. "What? What did Tamar want?" she demanded.

Dani looked stunned. "She thinks I did it."

"Oh no!" Her stomach plunge had been right.

"Because I was in the hall last night." Dani covered her face with her hands.

"But why? Why would you steal those things? You have no reason to take them!" Maya pulled Dani's hands from her face. She bent down to see into her friend's eyes. "What would Holmes say?" she demanded.

"H-he would say there's no motive." Dani's eyes were watery.

"That's right! There's no motive! And we're going to tell everyone that—including Tamar!"

"But what if no one believes me?"

"They will when we catch the thief—who is not you!" Maya clenched her teeth. There was a lot to do—thief-catching, justice-bringing. It was going to be a full day.

CHAPTER 14

"So, do you think they'll close camp if the thief is not found?" Marisa asked that afternoon during rest. They were supposed to be writing their twice-a-week letters home, but everyone kept getting distracted discussing the mystery. The golden light and pine-scented breeze filtered in through the screens, filling the cabin.

Marisa draped herself backward half off her bunk and tried to rest her pen under her nose. "I mean, Max sounded really serious." The pen clattered to the floor.

Yael was already done with her letter. It was folded neatly on her shelf, and now she was holding another sheet of paper in front of her face.

"Well, I think it's scary," Gracie added. She was writing busily on a sheet of stationery. Her mom must have packed it. Her pen had a big purple fluffball on the end. "What if the thief breaks in somewhere else?"

"I don't think that would really happen." Maya tapped her pen on the sheet of torn-out notebook paper resting on her bunk. She could never think of anything to say. *Hi, I'm fine, camp's fine. I'm still afraid of swimming. We have a thief at camp!* A nice uplifting letter like that?

Above her, Dani was silent. Maya could hear her pen scribbling away.

"I mean, who would *do* something like that?" Marisa was still talking. Her own sheet of paper was blank. "Like a psychopath? Someone who has no empathy for other people? *Stealing* Max's own grandfather's cup?"

"And candlesticks," Gracie reminded her. "Maybe the person really needs the money, and they want to sell them."

"Or maybe they hate their parents, and they need the money for bus fare to run away," Marisa said. "I saw that in a movie."

"I don't think people really take buses anymore like that," Maya said. "Anyway, I think it's really sick that no one has confessed." She glanced at the upper bunk. "Especially since anyone can be falsely accused."

Dani shifted above her but didn't say anything.

The clear, loud ringing of the bell above the dining hall sounded, signaling the end of rest time. Maya sat up, capped her pen, and stuffed her letter into an envelope. "I'm done," she said. "Give me your letters, guys. I'll collect them for Tamar."

Dani handed hers down from the upper bunk, and Marisa quickly started scribbling. Gracie flicked hers across the room.

"Yael, you want me to take yours?" Maya came over to her bunk and stopped. Yael hadn't heard her. She was whispering to herself, but she sounded weird—really shaky and kind of squeaky. "*Um*, Yael?"

Yael startled. "What?" She crumpled the paper in her hand.

"Your letter?" Maya asked hesitantly. "You want me to take it?"

"Oh! Yeah. Thanks." She took the folded letter from her shelf and thrust it at Maya.

Tamar stuck her head in the door.

"Got your letters, everyone? Hand them over—I'll put them in the mail this afternoon. Then we're going to have a group meeting with the Haifas and the Eilats before sports and games."

"I've got them, Tamar," Maya said. She handed them over amid the general bustle and chattering as everyone slid off their bunks.

Outside, Maya walked slowly along the path behind the others, letting the sounds of their conversation wash back over her. Something was going on with Yael. But what? That's what Maya didn't know.

"This theft is the most serious thing that has ever happened at Camp Shalom." Tamar looked around at the girls sitting in a circle around her on the grass of the East Meadow. "We don't want to get the police involved, but we will if we have to."

"That's right," the Eilat counselor put in. "We won't stop until we find the stolen items."

"We won't *stop*!" Cori sang out the lyrics to some song Maya didn't know. "Until we find love!" Her pith helmet was pushed back on her head, and she was as red-faced as ever. She caught Maya looking at her and winked. Maya looked away, annoyed she'd been caught staring.

"What would the police do?" Annie asked. She was sitting cross-legged, a chain of clover blossoms around her head.

"I don't know," Tamar said. "Possibly take the thief down to the station. After that, who knows?"

Maya gulped. That sounded really serious. Beside her, Dani stared at her lap, ashen-faced. Maya put her arm around her.

"Well, Dani found the challah cover and the candles," Gracie piped up. "Maybe the kiddush cup and the candlesticks will just turn up."

"Even if they do, someone will have still stolen them," Marisa said. "There would still be a thief out there."

"Oh yeah." Gracie looked deflated.

"I think it's scary," Rachel said. "I mean, if that person is among us, who really knows what they could do next? Where would they stop?" She looked around at each person in the group.

She doesn't sound the least bit scared, Maya thought. *She just likes the drama.*

Yael was silent, fiddling with the long braid that hung over one shoulder. Tamar fixed them all with another long stare. "I have only this to say, and then we're going to team sports. If the kiddush cup and candlesticks are not found by tomorrow, Max will call the police. If someone, anyone, has anything they want to say, they can tell me privately." She looked straight at Dani.

Everyone else did too. Maya could sense the energy in the room shifting. *Why was Tamar looking at Dani?* she could tell the others were thinking. Rachel leaned over and whispered to Cori. They both stared at Dani. Yael sorted through the tail of her braid for split ends.

"All right, that's it. Let's just hope someone comes forward," Tamar said. She got to her feet and the other counselors did too.

Halfway to the field, as they were passing the Arts and Crafts hut, Dani paused to take a twig out of her sneaker. Rachel fell in step with Maya. "So, who do you think the thief is?"

Maya glanced over at her. Her bouncy curls were

puffier than ever in the humid air, and the sides of her nose glistened greasily. "I don't know, obviously. No one does."

Rachel smirked. "Or you don't want to know."

"What?"

"It's obvious. Dani."

Maya forced herself to keep walking straight ahead, instead of tackling Rachel and pushing her face into the ground like she really wanted to. "Yeah? You think she's the one?"

"She probably 'found' the challah cover and candles just to throw everyone off the scent." Rachel raised her eyebrows. "That's a thing thieves do, you know."

"You're wrong." Maya looked straight ahead at the line of thick green trees marking the edge of the forest.

"You don't know that." Rachel's voice was infuriatingly smug.

"I *do*."

"How come?"

"She has no motive. There's no reason for her to take them." Maya ran ahead to the field where Greg the sports counselor was organizing them for a game of Dr. Dodgeball. Dani panted up beside her a minute later.

"What was Rachel talking to you about?" she asked, catching her breath.

"Nothing." Maya looped her arm through Dani's. "I hope you guys have fun at Snake Island without me."

"Stop! You're going to Snake Island, too, and we're going to share a tent. Remember? You. Are. Going." Dani scowled at Maya.

"All right, everyone, listen up!" Greg said. "Dr. Dodgeball is a Camp Shalom specialty. It's like an evil dodgeball, so I hope everyone's feeling devious."

"Me, obviously!" Yael giggled and flipped her braid back behind her shoulder.

"Great," Greg told her. "Your counselors are going to choose a secret doctor for each team. We've got Akko against Haifa up first. The winner will play Eilat. Now, don't let the other team know who your doctor is! If you get hit during the game, your doctor can tag you. Then you're back in. But if the other team figures out who your doctor is, they're definitely going to try to hit her, and then *she'll* be out. And remember—hits below the neck *only*." Greg clapped his hands together. "Let's go!"

The Akkos huddled around Tamar, sending suspicious glances at the Haifas, who were doing the same to their counselor. "Okay, who wants to be the doctor?" Tamar asked.

"Me! Me!" everyone started yelling.

"Gracie," Tamar whispered. "You be the doctor first."

Gracie grinned. "Got it."

Normally, Maya dreaded ball sports, especially volleyball—everyone looked at you while you served. She always whiffed and hit the air, and then everyone groaned, and then she had no choice but to die right there and never come back.

At least in dodgeball no one was really looking at you. And there was something strangely satisfying about hitting someone with a solid rubber-on-skin *thwack*. Everyone was yelling, and the yellow and green balls were flying back and forth and rolling across the asphalt square. "Dani, watch out!" Maya yelled as a green ball flew toward her friend. Dani danced aside and hit Annie square in the back with a yellow ball. Then Marisa got hit and froze.

"Gracie!" Yael almost yelled out before she clapped her hand over her mouth. Gracie scurried over to Marisa and tagged her on the back of the leg.

Then Maya saw a tall Haifa taking aim at her with a green ball. She squealed and dodged it, barely, then whipped around to see Dani taking a hit. "I'm frozen!" she called.

Across the line, Annie was still frozen too. Maya saw her motioning to someone. Rachel. Rachel was their Dr. Dodgeball. Rachel looked all around, and saw Maya watching her. Then she smirked—the same smirk she'd given Maya out in the meadow. Then she scooped up a green ball and turned to tag Annie.

Maya thought she might explode with hatred. She couldn't stop herself—she scooped up a yellow ball and fired it at Rachel as hard as she could—against the rules, of course. She aimed for her head—double-against the rules. The ball hit Rachel squarely in the back of her frizzy, puffy hair.

"*Oooowwww!*" she screamed, clutching the back of her head. "*Ooowww!* Someone hit me in the head. Greg! Someone hit me!" She staggered around—*as if she'd sustained a major brain injury, rather than a smack with a rubber ball*, Maya thought sourly.

Greg blew his whistle. "Time!" he called. "Maya, I saw that. You're out—this game and the next game. That was not good sportsmanship."

"Sorry!" Maya called. Maybe her voice sounded sorrier than she felt? Because she didn't feel the least bit sorry. In fact, she felt better than she'd felt all day.

"Nice shot!" Yael murmured as she passed her on the way to the sidelines. "I can't stand that girl."

"Me neither," Maya muttered back.

CHAPTER 15

"Why'd you do that to Rachel?" Dani asked afterward as they walked down the winding path to the lake. "She's so mad."

Maya looked at Rachel's rigid back, walking with Annie ahead of them. "Ah . . . I forgot. The rules. I forgot the rules."

Dani gave her a long look and a little smile. "Sure. They're pretty complicated, those Dr. Dodgeball rules."

Maya squeezed her friend's arm, but the sight of the lake drove all thoughts of Dr. Dodgeball out of Maya's head. The raft looked tiny as it bobbed like a little dry island in the middle of the vast expanse of dark brown-green water. Maya felt the familiar fear climbing into her throat as she stood on the shore with Dani beside her. All around her, happy campers were running into the woods to climb the ladder to the big slide or paddling in inner tubes or wrestling oars into the kayaks.

"Free swim, everyone!" Leah called from her perch on her lifeguard chair. Maya thought of everyone in their colorful canoes on their way to the Snake Island overnight. She thought of herself, waving them off, left behind. She must have heaved a sigh because Dani suddenly tugged at her arm.

"Forget this!" Dani said. "I'm not going to Snake Island without you! We're going to figure this out once and for all. Look, you can swim, right? It's not like you *can't* swim."

Maya nodded miserably. "I'm just not very good. I get in, and the water looks so dark and what if I drown and—"

"That's just your fear talking," Dani said.

"What?"

"That's what my dad always says. Are you talking or is it your fear?"

"Is this a pep talk?" Maya scowled at Dani. "I don't think I've told you I have kind of a thing against pep talks."

Dani ignored her, just like Mom always did. "We're going to do deep breathing."

"But—"

"Now, take a deep breath! Let it out!" Dani ordered.

Maya obeyed.

"How do you feel?"

She considered. A short way down the bank, Marisa let out a mighty shriek as she flew out the end of the slide and splashed into the water. "Freaked out," Maya said.

"Try again!"

Obediently, Maya inhaled and exhaled.

Dani watched her. "Feel calmer?"

"I feel the same! Can we go sit down now?" Maya pleaded.

"Definitely not! We're not sitting down until you swim to the raft!"

"Dani, stop." Yael suddenly pushed her way in between the two of them. She was holding two kickboards. "Just stop with the whole breathing thing. It's not working." She shoved one of her bobby pins deeper into her topknot. "I know what to do."

Oh no, what now? Maya thought.

"Maya doesn't need to be breathing deeply or whatever that was." Yael spoke with her usual confidence. She shoved one of the kickboards at Dani. "She needs support. We're going to go *with* her to the raft. And we won't let you drown, okay?" she said to Maya.

"*Um*, okay." Maya said uncertainly.

Yael put her arm around Maya's waist and, after a moment's hesitation, Dani did the same on the other side. Maya could feel the warmth coming off each of them. Their arms around her waist steadied her as they walked slowly deeper into the water. It almost felt like they were holding her.

One step. Then another. The murky water lapped around her knees. It looked like tea. "Okay?" Yael asked. Maya made her head nod.

"The lake is so big," she said uneasily.

"Just as big as it was before." Dani gripped her waist a little tighter. "Remember, you do know how to swim."

"And you're awesome at it!" Yael said a little loudly and not-totally-truthfully into Maya's right ear.

The water was up to her thighs now. Her legs disappeared into the murk. Her skin, when she glanced down, looked very white. She could see the goosebumps on her thighs. Something squished beneath her toes. "Is that mud?" She wobbled.

"Yep, just mud," Yael said. "It's good for your skin!"

Now they were up to their waists. She could feel the water trying to lift her off her feet. On either side, Dani and Yael kept a tight grip on her.

"Now, just lift your feet off. We'll let go. But we won't leave," Yael said. "We'll stay right here."

"*Whooaa . . .*" The water lapped against Maya's chest, pushing her.

"Come on!" Dani said. "You've got to try! You won't be alone."

Maya reached forward with her arms, like Leah had been reminding her to do. She let her feet lift off the bottom. Her heart was pounding in her ears. The surface of the water was so close to her face.

"Okay, now, we're going to let you go," Dani said.

Maya felt a stab of panic but fought it down and nodded. Their arms released. Maya stretched her arms out, taking another stroke.

On either side, Yael and Dani smiled at her, with wet hair slicked back and drops of lake water studding their cheeks, balancing their arms on their kickboards.

I'm not alone. Maya forced herself to think of Snake Island. She forced her arms to move. Then she felt herself slicing through the water. She was buoyant.

"Yeah!" Dani shrieked.

Maya spluttered, flapping, and snorting water. Her feet scrambled for the muddy bottom again. "You've got this!" Yael said, close to her. Her voice was low and calm. "Just keep reaching your arms out."

Maya forced herself to stretch out her arms. She started moving again.

"Nice, Maya!" Leah's voice floated from across the lake.

Maya looked across the rippling surface of the water. The raft looked so far away. "I can't make it," she groaned. Again, the deep water seemed to yawn beneath her, and panic rose up in her throat. "I can't," she repeated.

Yael swam even closer to her. She eased her kickboard

under one of Maya's arms. "Dani, support her on the other side," she ordered. Dani crowded against her.

"Here, just sort of lean on this," she said. She wedged the edge of her kickboard under Maya's other arm.

"We're with you," Yael said, close in her ear. "Just look at the raft."

The lake didn't seem so deep with them beside her. Maya could feel the panic ebbing. She fixed her eyes on the raft and kicked hard. Closer. They were getting closer. Then closer. She could see the slimy underside of the raft bobbing in front of her. It looked as big as a continent.

"Almost there!" Dani said. "Come on!"

Her legs were tired. She was almost there. Maya leaned forward on the sides of the kickboards and kicked her legs. Then she reached out and grasped the hard, solid wooden edge of the raft.

"OMG, you made it!" Dani squealed. She and Yael thrust the kickboards up onto the raft and hoisted themselves up.

"Here, grab my hand," Yael said, leaning down and extending a wet arm. Together, she and Dani dragged Maya up onto the gorgeous, glorious, warm, dry, solid surface of the raft.

"You did it!" Yael shrieked, throwing her arms around Maya and squeezing her hard. "I can't believe it."

"I did it," Maya repeated. She couldn't believe those

words were actually coming out of her mouth. "I really did."

"Yes! You did!" Dani squeezed her from the other side. "I knew you could!"

"*Whoa.*" Maya sprawled out on her back, the warm, hard boards feeling better than the best bed she'd ever slept in. She gazed up at the crystal-blue sky arching endlessly above her. Her arms ached. Her legs muscles were popping with little pings. Dani lay down next to her and Yael was on her other side. For a time, none of them spoke, they just lay there with their eyes closed. Then Maya raised her head. "You know the reason I got here?"

"Because you're a ferocious tiger-lady?" Dani spoke without opening her eyes, her hands crossed loosely on her chest like a mummy's.

"No." Maya pushed herself up. She'd left a head and torso-shaped wet mark on the boards. "Because you were there. Both of you. I never could have done it without the kickboard trick, Yael."

Yael opened her eyes and smiled. "My mom used to do that when I was learning to swim. I remember it made me feel better too."

"Well, it was freaking brilliant, and there's no way I'd be lying here now if it weren't for you."

They lay there a long time, feeling the sun warming their skin and the boards go dry under them. The way back didn't seem so long either, not with the kickboards—and her friends—beside her. But the question was, could she make it without them?

When the three of them finally staggered in from the lake, triumphant, dripping, with Dani and Yael clutching the slimy kickboards, Leah greeted them on the sand. "Really excellent strokes there! I see you had some good help."

Dani and Yael grinned.

"I didn't feel as scared with them there," Maya said. She threw her friends a grateful look.

"Another round of swim tests are tomorrow," Leah said. "To be honest, I wasn't sure how they were going to go for you, but I think you might have had a bit of a breakthrough. How about coming down after dinner tonight for a private lesson with me? Now that I've seen what you need, I bet I can help you. You might be surprised at how much progress you can make."

"Yeah!" Yael smacked Maya's shoulder with surprising strength.

"Do it, Maya!" Dani chimed in.

"Okay," Maya said slowly. Maybe Leah was right. She *did* feel a little better now.

"This is all because of you guys," Maya told them as they toweled off. "If you hadn't gotten me into the water, Leah wouldn't be offering me extra help."

Dani grinned. But Yael didn't look at either of them. She was examining a frayed edge to her towel. Then suddenly, without saying anything, she wrapped the towel around herself and dashed away.

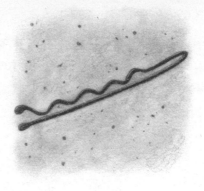

CHAPTER 16

Tamar gave her permission to have the extra swim lesson, so after dinner, Maya found Leah by the lake. The air was soft and mellow, and the slanting sun threw golden rays across the rippling surface of the water. "I watched what your friends were doing earlier today," Leah said. "Having them right beside you in the water seemed to really help you, didn't it? You were leaning on the kickboard, but I don't think you actually need it to stay afloat. It just made you feel supported, right? No pun intended."

"Yes." Maya took a deep breath. During dinner, she'd decided what she was going to say. Briefly, she outlined what happened when Miles pushed her into the pool. "I was all alone in the pool, and I kept coming up and seeing kids on the surface and thinking, *Why won't they help me? Don't they see I'm drowning?* I felt so alone. When

I get in now, it's like all I can think of is how I might drown alone again, and I get so scared, I forget about swimming. But when Yael and Dani were with me today, I didn't feel alone. So I didn't feel so scared."

Leah smiled. "Maya, I can't even tell you how glad I am that you told me this. I didn't know what the problem was before, so I couldn't help you! Now I know, and I'm not going to leave you either—just like your friends."

For the next hour, Leah showed Maya how to do a self-rescue anytime she felt unsafe in the water; the main thing was to roll on her back and float while she collected herself. That would give her time to catch her breath and calm down if she got scared. Then they swam together, with Leah right beside Maya. They practiced with Leah moving a little farther away, then a little farther, until she was out of arm's reach. Maya's anxious heart wasn't even pounding by the time Leah stopped swimming with her.

"I'm doing it!" Maya gasped, churning her arms through the dark water. "I'm really doing it!"

"Maya," Leah said solemnly. "You're more than doing it. Look ahead."

Maya lifted her head and gasped. The wooden edge of the raft loomed. Just like before—but this time she wasn't leaning on a kickboard. She wasn't leaning on anything. Three more strokes. Two more. And her hand grasped the silvery, dry edge. With Leah beside her, Maya hauled herself up onto the warm planks and flopped over on her back. The relief was tremendous.

"Leah," Maya said, "do—do you think I can pass the swim test? I mean, you won't be in the water with me."

Leah had pulled herself up on the raft, too, and now she was sitting on the edge, her legs dangling in the water. She smiled at Maya. "I really think you can. You have to be brave! But after what you did tonight, I really think you can."

Back on the shore, Maya wrapped her towel around her shoulders, shivering. The sun had dropped and already dusk was gathering among the trees. Leah's radio crackled to life. "Leah." Olivia's voice came through the speaker. "Joel sliced his hand on the hedgehog cage. Can you come provide first aid?"

Leah rolled her eyes. "That's like the third time Joel's bled this session. You'd think the guy would be more careful. I better get up there—go straight back to the bunk, okay?"

"Okay," Maya said, trying to dust the sand off her feet before she strapped on her sandals. "Thank you for the extra help. I'm feeling a lot better."

"Good." Leah crunched up the trail.

Maya lay on her stomach on the sand for a minute, resting. It felt so good to lie there on the warm sand, with no one around, and think about going on the sleepover. Idly, she replayed the swim lesson in her mind. *Tomorrow, I just have to remember that I'm not alone. No one's going to leave me to drown. I can swim.* Maya turned her head away from the setting sun and pressed her cheek to the sand. The beach looked different from this perspective. She could see all the rises and dips of the ground, like they were mountains and valleys. If she were an ant, that's what the ground would be like.

Then suddenly, she squinted. Footprints. There were footprints far at the end of the beach, but she could see them from where she was. They led from the steep bank that sloped from the woods and marked the end of the beach to a shed about ten feet from the bank. She sat up. The footprint trail disappeared. She flattened herself to the ground, cheek to the sand, and looked sideways. Her mother always did this when she was looking for broken glass after something fell in the kitchen. It was how she'd found her sister's glasses lens when it fell in the grass. And the trick worked here too. The footprint trail was visible again.

Maya shot up and ran over to the edge of the beach, tripping over roots. No one went to this end of the beach—she didn't even know where the trail leading down from the bank started. And the footprint trail was gone, but when she dropped down again and pressed her face to the sand, it was back. It led right to an old shed that stood pressed back against the brambly bushes that had crept their way down from the forest to the beach.

Maya didn't even remember anyone going near the shed during swimming. The oar house was on the other side of the beach. This was some crumbling old structure with splintery green-painted boards and dust-coated windows. But someone had been over here, and recently enough to leave footprints. Trying not to step on the footprints—Holmes would definitely not approve of messing up the evidence with one's own foot, very undetective-like—Maya wrestled with the rusty latch. It pulled back with a screech, and she pried open the heavy wooden door. Inside was cool and dark and smelled like mud and plant rot. Maya fumbled for a light switch before realizing there wasn't one, and then shoved the door open as wide as she could to let in the golden, slanting rays of the setting sun.

Rough shelves lined both walls, crammed with paint cans, ropes, discarded kickboards from some earlier years of camp, a dusty first-aid kit, old-fashioned looking paddles. An ancient-looking wooden canoe sat on the floor at her feet. Maya shifted her feet. Sand gritted underneath. She lowered herself to the floor again, despite the dirt and old spiderwebs, and turned her head sideways. There was the sand again, scattered across the floor like sugar. It led in a trail to the one of the shelves.

Someone had tracked it on her shoe. Someone had been in here. Suddenly, Maya thought of the trail of mulch in the bunk after opening ceremonies. Mulch. Where had she seen mulch before? Then she knew. The red mulch that covered the ground of the amphitheater. Trail of mulch in the bunk. Trail of sand here.

Maya jumped to her feet and began pawing through the cluttered shelf nearest to the sand trail. She shoved aside heavy cans of paint, rusty tackle from fishing rods, and a coil of mildewed rope. Then her fingers touched something smooth and cool.

The kiddush cup and the candlesticks. Maya pulled them out and looked at them. The worn old silver gleamed pink in the light from the setting sun streaming through the door. She had to tell Dani! And Tamar, and everyone else. Maya turned to run from the shed but then stopped herself.

She may have found the cup and the candlesticks, but she hadn't found the thief. She had to look for clues. Slowly, Maya walked from the shed, head down, scanning the ground. The thief came in here, and the footprint trail led from the shed to the far end of the beach, about ten feet away. Maya shuffled along the ground, scanning for signs of anything strange. She held the precious silver objects tightly against her chest. The sand was all churned up and when she carefully lowered herself to ground level again, she could see that the footprint trail led straight to a small dirt path she'd never noticed before.

It was barely a path—more like an opening in the scrubby bushes that led down to the beach. But whoever made the footprint path must have come this way. The rest of the lakeshore was an impenetrable tangle of brambles and bushes until the strip of yellow sand took over.

Her heart beating faster, Maya slowly climbed the steep bank. Far away, she could hear the bell calling everyone to start evening campfire. It seemed like it was on another planet. Here, there was only her own breath in her ears, the heavy silver pressed to her chest and the brambles scratching her legs. She fixed her eyes on the ground. The path rose steeply, and she could feel the muscles in her legs straining.

Then a gleam of something straight and black leaped out at her. As she swooped down to grab it, she recognized what it was. A bobby pin.

CHAPTER 17

Maya thought the cabin would be deserted when she pushed open the screen door. Everyone should be at the evening campfire. The dusky room sat as if it were waiting, with a soft breeze wafting through the screens. Each bed was neatly made. All the clothes were put away.

Then something stirred at the far end of the room, and Maya saw Yael lying in her bed, completely covered, with her sleeping bag pulled over her head.

As gently as she could, Maya put the kiddush cup and candlesticks down on Tamar's footlocker. They clanked a little and Yael raised her head, clawing back the sleeping bag. She saw the objects. Maya saw her spot them. For a long moment, they both stared—Yael at the objects, and Maya at Yael.

Then Yael flopped back down on her pillow. "Cool,

you found them," she said. She drew the sleeping bag up under her nose.

"Yeah. They were, *um*, in the shed on the beach." What was she supposed to do now?

"Great. I guess we can lead Shabbat then." Yael turned over, her body a long hump under the sleeping bag.

Maya remained standing uncertainly in the middle of the floor. "How come you're not at the campfire?"

"Sick." Yael's voice was muffled now. "My head's killing me."

"Oh." Now what? How do you just say, *Um, may I accuse you of a crime, please*?

Then Maya thought of what to do. With her heart thumping in her ears, she walked up next to Yael and without saying anything, placed the bobby pin on her pillow.

Yael's eyes popped open like window shades, and she stared at the pin. A hand snaked out from under the sleeping bag and took the pin. "Thanks." The sleeping bag stayed covering half her face.

Maya sat down at the foot of Yael's bed. The springs creaked under her weight. She didn't say anything. Neither did Yael. The silence stretched out. Outside the screens, two birds were having a noisy argument. Maya could hear heart pounding in her ears. Prickles ran up and down her body. Yael was the thief. But was she bad?

A liar and a criminal? *She helped me swim. She fixed my hair. But she was so mean on the bus, too. . . . Why would she do this? Why would she steal something valuable and hide it?*

Yael still didn't move. Maya felt frozen to the side of the bed. She didn't want to say anything first. But Yael's silence was starting scare her. Why didn't she move? Why didn't she say anything? What if the others came back and found them like this, with the candlesticks and the cup just sitting on the end of the bed?

Yael sat up abruptly. Her hair was matted and tangled on one side. "All right! All right! I did it, okay? I know you know, and now I'm saying it! I did it, and I'm sorry! I'll start packing now." She threw back the sleeping bag and dragged her duffel bag from under her bed.

Still talking, she started throwing T-shirts and shorts into it. "I'm a thief! Sue me! I was desperate, okay? I've never done anything like that before and I never will again, but that doesn't matter, does it? You're going to tell Tamar and Max, and I'll be out of here and I can never come back to Shalom again. Fine!" She zipped the duffel with difficulty and tried to pull it across the room.

"Well, I'm not going to tell Tamar," Maya said uneasily. Wait. That wasn't want she meant to say. She wasn't going to tell Tamar? Really? And let Tamar think that Dani did it? "But, *um*, why did you do it?"

"Why? Why?" Yael stopped tugging at the trunk. "Because I can't read out loud! I just can't—I've never been able to. It's a phobia, okay? My voice goes all squeaky and wobbly, and it feels like my stomach's jumped up into my throat to choke me." She grabbed a book from Dani's bed, opened it and peered at it. She snapped it closed. "Nope! Can't do it." She said the words as if pronouncing something disgusting.

Maya stood silently, watching.

Yael kept yelling. "I couldn't stand it, all this practicing to lead Shabbat. I wasn't going to be able to stand up there and read. I wasn't going to be able to do it. Practicing with you guys was bad enough. Then let's just complete the humiliation by showing the whole camp that I can't read out loud without sounding like a baby. Like a loser." Yael was pacing back and forth, tears flowing down her face. She spat her words. Fury was rolling off her in waves. Maya could see the tendons in her neck. "Do you know what it feels like not to be able to do something literally everyone else can do? Do you? No, I don't think you do. None of you do, all you happy, silly girls prancing around . . . none of you know what it feels like!"

"Actually, I do," Maya said. Her hands were clammy and she was still scared, but the words poured out of her anyway. "Have you completely forgotten that I could barely swim when I got here? And that I was—I guess I still am—afraid of *water*?" Her voice rose. "I walked around feeling like a baby too! Like I had this huge dumb secret—not even a good secret, just a stupid secret!" She stopped. Yael was staring at her.

"It's the same. . . ." Yael said slowly.

Maya stared back. "Yeah. It is." They both had secrets and fears, she and Yael. Except Yael had helped with hers. Maya sat back down on the bunk.

"So . . . how did you do it?" Maya asked carefully. She didn't want to upset the delicate calm they seem to have achieved.

Yael sank back down on the bunk beside her. She sighed and twiddled a loose thread between her fingers. "I took the practice stuff out of the trunk when everyone was at the opening ceremony. I just pretended I was going to bathroom and then ran back really quickly. I thought maybe if the stuff was gone, we couldn't practice, and they'd find another bunk to lead Shabbat."

Maya remembered Yael coming back to the amphitheater at the campfire that first day, all red in the face and Tamar telling her she had to stay with the group. "The mulch on the floor of the cabin. . ." Maya said, piecing things together.

"Yeah. I guess I tracked it in. It kind of clings to the bottom of your shoes."

"But the candlesticks and the kiddush cup . . ." Maya said. They both looked at the jumble of silver lying on Tamar's trunk.

Yael exhaled. "Yeah. I was feeling pretty desperate. It

was obvious Tamar was going to make us go ahead with leading the service. I thought maybe if I stomped on the whole Shabbat spirit enough, they'd just forget about it." She put her face in her hands and leaned her elbows on her knees. "Stupid, stupid, stupid." Her voice was muffled, but Maya could understand her anyway. "I took it that day in the dining hall when we were all singing 'If I Had a Hammer.' It was easy. Everyone was making so much noise I could just slip away and unlock Max's door. I was back before you all even realized I was gone."

Maya crouched down in front of Yael. "Listen. You have to know something. Tamar suspects Dani. I can't say why exactly, but Dani was in the right place to have stolen the things at the right time. Tamar hasn't said anything outright, but if she tells Max about her suspicions, they might send Dani home."

Yael jerked her hands out of Maya's. "No! I'm sorry, Maya. I wasn't thinking about anything like that."

You sure weren't, Maya thought.

"I never thought Dani would get involved," Yael twirled one of her bobby pins around and around between her fingers. "What am I going to do?"

Maya sat very still on the bunk. She knew what had to happen. But she didn't know how it was going to happen.

Out on the path, they heard the laughing and

shrieking of the Akkos coming up from the campfire. Maya could see the bobbing of their flashlights on the trail.

"They're here," she said.

Yael nodded. Her eyes were huge. "Okay," she whispered.

Gracie and Marisa were shrieking with laughter as they came in, with Dani and Tamar behind them, but everyone stopped when they took in the scene: Yael standing in the middle of the room, Maya on the bunk with her head bowed, the jumble of silver on Tamar's trunk.

"Maya?" Marisa gasped. "You?"

Tamar started to speak, but Yael broke in. "Wait, please, everyone. I have something to tell you."

Tamar looked like she wanted to speak but changed her mind. Her eyes flew from the silver to Maya to Yael to Dani and back. Everyone sank down on their bunks.

"I'm the thief," Yael said simply. "It was me. Me all along. I stole the practice stuff. I stole the kiddush cup and candlesticks from Max's office. Just me, no one else."

Everyone gasped. Relief flooded Maya. She felt like cheering. Her eyes met Dani's, who mimed fainting with relief.

Tamar's face was astonished. "You, Yael? But I thought—"

"Please wait," Yael almost whispered. "I have to get through this, and it's really hard." Briefly and simply, she explained to the group what she'd told Maya—hiding the practice items, then stealing and hiding the silver. By the time she was finished, she was almost whispering into her lap.

"So you didn't have to read out loud?" Marisa asked.

Yael lifted her tear-streaked face. "You've never stood up in front of everyone and had your voice shaking like a baby, have you? I've tried and tried. Everyone says I'll get better. But it doesn't feel like it."

Maya pushed her way over to Yael. She put her arm around her and faced the others. "Listen, I have something to say." She met each of their stares with her own. "I'm not saying that stealing the stuff was okay. Obviously, it wasn't. But I've had a secret, too, this session—you guys know it now. All my trouble with swimming. I've been so scared of the water, just like Yael is scared of reading out loud, and Yael and Dani helped me. They really, really helped me. So I say that now's our turn to help Yael. Somehow."

Everyone was silent. "I agree," Dani spoke up.

Marisa turned to Tamar. "Can we? Does Yael have to get in trouble?"

Tamar sighed. "Girls, I don't know. Yael, I'm glad you've told us the truth. We can see how upset you are.

But the fact is that you took these things, and without Maya, they would have stayed lost. We'll have to go talk to Max in the morning." Her tough face cracked into a smile. "But I hear you. If there's any way to help our Akko, we'll do it."

CHAPTER 18

"Yes! Maya, go!" Dani, Gracie, and Marisa screamed the next day. Yael and Tamar had been in the office with Max all morning. Leah had been the one to fetch them for the swim tests.

Maya churned her arms through the water. The lake water splashed in her face. Her legs were getting tired. Ahead of her, she could see the edge of the raft, rocking slightly in the water. She could get there. Could she get there?

"I'm here with you, Maya," Leah said. She was treading water with her, floating just a few feet away. "I'm not going to let anything happen to you. If you get tired, just do a self-rescue. You know how to help yourself."

I can do it. I'm not alone. I can do it. I'm not alone. Maya kept her eyes fixed on the raft. *Snake Island, Snake*

Island, Snake Island, she said like a chant in her head. She pictured Dani and Yael in the water beside her. Her friends were with her. No one would let anything bad happen to her.

"I need a break," she gasped suddenly. She rolled on her back like Leah had taught her and stared at the sky. Puffy blue clouds floated overhead.

"Breathe slowly," Leah said.

Maya tried. Gradually her breath came back. She rolled back on her stomach in the water and struck out again with a building feeling of triumph. She'd done a self-rescue! She hadn't even come close to panicking! The raft was growing closer with every stroke.

A little more. Then a little more, and suddenly just as she grasped the splintery wooden edge, another voice joined in the cheering from the shore. "Yes, Maya!" Yael screamed.

Panting, Maya hoisted herself onto the raft, and looked back. Yael was standing on the shore now too. "I did it!" she shouted back at her fellow Akkos. They were all jumping and screaming. Maya looked at Leah, floating in the water. She was grinning too.

"I guess you're going to Snake Island," Leah called out.

"Yes, I am!" Maya screamed. She'd done it. But not without a whole lot of help from her friends.

Back on the shore, everyone was clustered around

Yael. "Hurry up!" Dani shouted as Maya shivered her way out of the water, wrapping a towel around her shoulders. "Yael won't tell us what happened until you're here."

"I'm here!" Maya ran up.

"Okay, well," Yael began. "I told Max everything, and Tamar was there and two of the board members. It was kind of scary. But then Tamar told everyone how I'd helped Maya and how Maya had spoken up for me last night. She said it showed that we Akkos were helping each other. They were all listening really carefully, and when I was done, they went off and had a private conference, and I was sure that was it, they were calling my parents and, possibly, the police."

"And?" Marisa asked.

"And then they came back and said that I could be on probation, and I have one more chance. We're still going to do Shabbat, but Tamar said you guys would help me, so will you?" she finished in a rush, looking around the group.

"Of course, we will!" Maya said right away. "I just passed my swim test because you and Dani helped me! Now it's our turn." She looked around the group.

"Yes!" Dani said. Everyone else nodded.

Maya caught Dani's eye and grinned. "After all," Maya said. "You won't be alone."

CHAPTER 19

"Maya, where's my brush? Have you seen my hairbrush?" Dani was on her knees, rummaging in the giant duffel bag at the end of their bunk beds.

"No, and I just stepped on my dress." Maya picked her sundress off the floor and scrubbed at the footprint now gracefully arrayed across the front. "Maybe people will think it's part of the pattern."

The cabin was full of slanting evening light and soft pine air. And something else, too, Maya thought, as she looked around at her bunkmates slipping on dresses and searching for sandals. A kind of quiet, peaceful excitement for the start of Shabbat.

It was almost time. Maya caught Yael's eye across the room. Her friend came over with a wet washcloth. "Here, I can get that off," she said. She scrubbed at the footprint.

"It's going to be okay." Maya caught at Yael's hand as she turned away. "We've got a plan."

Yael tried to smile. "I know. I'm still a little nervous."

"We've got this," Maya said.

Dani emerged from her duffel bag with her hairbrush in hand. "We definitely do," she echoed.

Gracie and Marisa turned from their bunks too. "Akkos together," Gracie said.

"Akkos together," Maya echoed and put her arms around Dani on one side and Marisa on the other. The others draped their arms around each other's shoulders, too, and they stood in a circle together, swaying slightly with the first chirps of the evening crickets coming in through the door.

"Time to go, girls," Tamar said softly, and they tramped out of the cabin. Maya looked back as the screen door swung shut. Each bed was neatly covered with its sleeping bag, and the towels were folded over the ends. All the clothes that were normally strewn on the floor were picked up and stowed in the duffel bags. Beside Tamar's bed was a little vase of daisies they'd picked on the way back home from lunch.

"Like home," Dani said beside her. Maya realized she'd been looking at the room too.

"I never thought I'd hear you say that," Maya said. "But I was thinking the same thing."

"I know." Dani linked her arm with Maya's as they

went down the steps together. "Weird, right? You make enough friends and go through enough stuff together and then . . . I don't know . . . the place where your friends are starts seeming like home."

Maya thought of Yael and Dani paddling on their kickboards beside her like faithful mermaids. "'The place where your friends are . . .'" she echoed. The lake might not feel *exactly* like home yet. But it didn't feel like enemy territory any longer.

Outside, the path was filling with campers streaming from their bunks, girls with hair wet from their showers, in dresses and skirts. They all walked together toward the lake, everyone with their arms around each other, laughing and talking.

Some people were already gathering on the benches that surrounded the amphitheater stage. The lake in front of them rippled in the night breeze, edged in gray and pink from the setting sun. Tamar was saving seats for them in the front. Maya followed Dani down the row.

"*Psst!*" someone said behind her.

She turned around. Cori was filing into the row behind them along with the other Eilats. "You guys thought we stole the candlesticks and stuff." For once she wasn't wearing her pith helmet. Her hair was sort of slapped to her head with water.

"Yeah, sorry about that," Maya whispered.

"Accident," Dani added.

Cori and the buzz-cut Eilat glanced at each other. "And we got in trouble for the shaving cream. Maybe one of you told on us."

"No, I didn't!" Maya said.

"Or me!" Dani said behind her.

Cori grinned fiendishly. "Well, guess what? We're going with you on the Snake Island trip. There's going to be some payback."

Maya stared at her until Marisa bumped her. "Tamar says sit down," Marisa whispered.

Maya sat. "That is not going to be good," she said to Dani, in a low voice.

"You think?" Dani murmured back.

Gracie leaned over. "Dani! Maya! It's us first!"

Up on the stage, Maya could see Max and Josh and Olivia and Leah—all the activities counselors—everyone dressed in white shirts. On a little table stood the silver candlesticks and the kiddush cup. "You guys ready?" Tamar asked.

Dani nodded. Yael did, too, but her eyes were huge and scared. Maya squeezed Yael's hand. "Remember our plan," she told her. "You can do this."

"Shabbat shalom, campers," Max's voice drifted out over the campers.

All the chatter died away, and silence fell over the campers. Maya felt her heart quicken in anticipation. "Will the Akkos come up, please, to lead us in the candle-lighting, kiddush, and opening readings?" Max asked, smiling. He gestured at the front row. Maya's heart gave a big skip. This was it. She glanced over at Yael, whose face was pale and sweaty.

Together, they rose. Tamar grinned at them from her seat. "Good luck, girls!" she whispered. "You can do this!"

They made their way up onto the stage. *The crowd looks so much bigger from up here*, Maya thought. The faces swam in front of her. Behind her, she could hear Yael breathing fast. Dani stood on one side and Marisa on the other. Gracie stood beside Marisa. The campers rustled around expectantly, and then silence fell. They were waiting.

The silver candlesticks and the kiddush cup gleamed on the table in front of them as if they'd never been gone. Someone—Max, maybe?—had polished them until they shone with a mellow glow. The kiddush cup was already filled with grape juice. A box of matches lay beside the candlesticks.

Maya heard Yael swallow. Then she picked up the matches, the way they'd practiced. A little rustle went through the staff. No doubt they knew how the candlesticks and the cup had returned. Yael's fingers were shaking, but she struck the match and touched the little yellow flame to the wicks.

"*Baruch ata Adonai . . .*" the Akkos recited together.

"*Eloheinu melech ha-olam . . .*" Their voices, tentative at first, gained strength, until Maya knew even the campers in the back row could hear them.

After they finished the blessing over the candles, Marisa picked up the kiddush cup. The old silver gleamed in the warm light from the candles. Maya thought of what a long journey that cup had had—from Europe to Max's grandfather's house, then to its home in the office, then the boatshed—and now, finally, here—back where it belonged. "*Baruch ata Adonai . . .*" they all recited again, "*Eloheinu melech ha-olam borei p'ri hagafen!*"

Marisa took a sip from the cup. Then she set it down. Dani nudged Maya in the side. She swallowed hard and stepped forward. "*Um.*" *Not a great opening, but go with it.* "Normally, each person in the cabin reads a poem now. But, *um*, we wanted to do something different. So we're going to recite our poem together." Why did her voice keep going up at the end like that? Anyway, it was over. Max was nodding.

"Great! Go ahead, Akkos," he said.

Maya stepped back into line and grabbed Yael's hand. She heard a murmuring from the assembled campers. Everyone else joined hands, too, just like they'd practiced. "Go!" she whispered.

"*Evening stars glint in the sky,*" they recited together.

"*It's time to welcome the Sabbath bride.*

Into the night, the sparks fly high."

Their voices smoothed out and blended together.

"Our candlelight touches each inside.

The wine we drink warms each of us,

Bring us close in togetherness.

We see campers sitting side by side . . ."

They fell silent, as they had practiced. Maya glanced over at Yael. She was staring at her feet. "You can do this!" Maya murmured. "We're here with you." She squeezed Yael's hand. The others looked over, nodding and smiling.

Yael looked at them. Then she straightened her back and nodded. *"Love . . ."* she began alone, and her voice cracked.

Come on! Maya thought.

Yael cleared her throat and her voice grew stronger. *". . . Love and friendship in their eyes."*

There was a moment of quiet, and then Max stepped forward. "Thanks, Akkos. That was really special."

"You guys were great!" Tamar whispered to them as they found their seats together. "I knew you could do it!" She looked at Yael. "And you were Akkos together. I'm proud of you."

"Are you guys glad it's all over?" Dani asked later as the Akkos scuffed slowly to the chadar ochel after services. The Shabbat dinner would be waiting there, with turkey and rolls and carrots all laid out on the long tables.

They'd make *hamotzi* and eat together, then sing into the night. Full darkness had fallen, and the stars were flung across the black stretch of sky like handfuls of dust and glitter. *Evening stars glint in the sky*, Maya thought. There was some magic here.

"Is camp magic a thing?" she asked aloud, head tilted back.

"Camp magic?" Marisa said. "What's that?"

"You know . . . like some kind of stew made of friends and singing and that sound the cabin door makes when it slaps shut." Maya stopped suddenly, embarrassed. Maybe no one else felt that way.

"Yeah," Dani said. She looped her arm with Maya's. "I know what camp magic is."

"What?" Yael asked.

"It's friends together always."

Ahead of them, the dining hall glowed warm and bright. The Akkos went up the steps together, leaving the still, starry night behind.

ACKNOWLEDGEMENTS

I'm so grateful to everyone who helped this book come to life. Catriella Freedman and PJ Library supported me from the very beginning and provided many notes on many drafts, as well as retreat space in which to work. Max Yamson at Camp Livingston told me all about life at Jewish summer camp, and so did my camper consultants, Henry Bernay and Greg Kleinschmidt. Thank you for letting me pick your brains. My agent Michael Bourret and my editor Brett Duquette were incredibly, persistently upbeat and encouraging, as was the team at Little Bee, including Kristin Errico, Natalie Padberg Bartoo, Paul Crichton, Tristan Lueck, and Alli Brydon. Kayla Stark's illustrations beautifully illuminated the text. Thank you to all the friends who shared their camp memories with me. And to my husband Aaron, and my three boys—thank you for giving the best hugs and being the best cheerleaders I could ever have.